WAITING
AND OTHER STORIES

Joseph L. Richardson

WAITING
And other stories
Copyright Joseph L. Richardson, 2015
All Rights Reserved

The events and characters in this book
are fictitious. Certain real locations and
public figures are mentioned, but all other
characters and events described in the book
are totally imaginary.

Published in the United States of America.

ISBN – 9781512196092
EAN - 9781512196092

No part of this book may be reproduced in any form unless written permission is granted from the author except for small portions to promote it. No electronic reproduction, information storage, or retrieval systems may be used or applied to any part of this book without written permission from the author

To order copies of this book or to provide reviews, please visit Amazon.Com. It can also be ordered by your local bookstore.

Jrichard35@cfl.rr.com

CONTENTS

Pieces of the Wall	7
Hush Little Baby	11
The Lighthouse	15
To be Read in Black and White only	21
I Never Had a Daughter	23
Grandmother	25
Parade	29
The Man in Gray	31
Sticks	35
The Smell of Pine	43
Ella Jean	45
The Movement of Life	49
Waiting	53
Between Abelard and Zola	57
The Artwork	75
Dowd's War	77
The Theory	79
Tunnels	85
Morning Mist	89
The Readin'	91
Poems	97
Halloween 1939	99
The Best Laid Plan	105
Old Tom and Twinkleberry	115
More Poems	119
Mrs. Bailey's Butterbeans	121
A Few More Poems	129
The Black Box	131
My Criminal Past	135
Golden Anniversary	139
The Winemakers	147
Stand Up	153
When You're a Man	161

Dreams of a Sixteen-Year-Old	171
The Hitchhiker	173
The Last of the Red Hot Marbles	175
When Florida Folks Pulled the Old Man's Beard for a living	183
A streetcar called Jungle	187

Where do ideas for stories come from?

Every day story hints come to us by way of our five senses. Most ignore them. Others see in them as potential subjects for their writing. They twist, turn, change, and build on them until they become stories that others will read and enjoy and will fulfill the creative hunger of the writer. Many of the best hints come from our eighth or ninth sense, our memory of things--good and bad—from the past.

Pieces of the Wall

"Pieces of the wall!" the man shouted in a heavily accented voice. "Get pieces of the wall right here!"

He stood at the side of the road, his hands and face grimy and his clothing soiled from his work. On the ground beside him was a twice-gray blanket, once from the dull color of the original weave and again from the dirt of the odd-shaped pieces of stone arranged in neat rows upon it.

"Piece of the wall, Mister?" he asked again. "Want to buy a piece of the wall?"

My trip had been long and tiring. My funds had been limited, so I had stayed several nights in small inns that were crowded and did not offer the best or most restful accommodations, but I had vowed that I would make the trip to see where the wall had stood until only weeks before. The wall had served not only as a divider between peoples, but also as a symbol of the differences in their beliefs.

I stepped close to the man and his wares. The pieces of stone ranged from the size of my thumb to the size of my hand. I picked up two of the smaller ones and studied their rough, gray surfaces. "So, these are from the wall," I said, half to the man and half to myself.

"Yes Sir. Those are pieces that I retrieved from the rubble. I broke them into smaller pieces so that they would be easier for a person to handle...and to make it easier for a person to take them home as souvenirs.

I glanced up at the man and saw the kind of smile that begs confidence when its wearer seeks acceptance of words that tend to stretch the truth. Oh, yes, I thought, broken into pieces for the convenience of the buyer...the more pieces, the more sales. Those larger, hand sized pieces will undoubtedly be broken into smaller, "easier to handle" pieces as his inventory is depleted.

"I was there," he said, his chest swelling. "Yes, Sir, I was right there when the wall came down. Saw it with my own eyes! Got these pieces right then. Knew a lot of people would want souvenirs, but would not be able to get them for themselves. I can give you a good price on those two you are holding."

"It must have been very exciting when the wall came down," I said.

"Oh yes, very exciting indeed. There was a great deal of shouting and people were blowing horns. It certainly was exciting. I have never seen anything like it. The crowds were there for a week ...a whole week ...marching and shouting, and blowing horns! You know," he continued, his voice softening, "when that wall came down it ended years of separation…many years of separation.

I looked at the two pieces in my hand, and then back at the man. "How much for these two pieces," I asked considering one for my brother and one for myself.

He named his price for the two.

I rubbed my fingers against the rough hardness of the stones and thought how foolish I had been to inquire, knowing that I had barely funds for a few skimpy meals and the trip home.

"I'm sorry," I said. "The price is reasonable, I suppose, for a souvenir that represents something of such historical significance, but I simply can't afford it."

"I'm sorry," I repeated as I looked into the sad, brown eyes that told me that the man understood... that he was no better off than I. I stooped and replaced the pieces of stone on the blanket in as near their original positions as I could remember. I straightened and we looked at each other for a long moment. Then, he knelt and rearranged the two pieces, each a fraction of an inch.

As I walked away I turned and looked back at the man who wore soiled robes and worn sandals and who, once again, was loudly announcing his wares.

"Pieces of the wall!" he shouted. "Get pieces of the wall! Right here. Pieces of the wall of Jericho!"

Hush Little Baby, Hush

"Hush little baby, don't you cry," his mother sang to him as he lay in his crib. "Hush, now. Hush," she urged.

"Children were meant to be seen and not heard," his grandmother told him whenever he babbled something as a tot.

NEVER SPEAK UNLESS SPOKEN T0.

"Shut up. Stop that damned racket," his grandfather growled when he talked too loudly.

"That is enough out of you, young man. Now you will write I WILL NOT TALK one hundred times on the blackboard," his teacher admonished.

"Don't talk back to me!" his father shouted, a threatening hand raised.

ONE PICTURE IS WORTH A THOUSAND WORDS.

"Shhh. Shhh," his mother hissed. "I'm watching my soap opera."

"Um," said his father through his newspaper when the boy wanted to tell him something important.

He sat in the back row in class and never volunteered an answer. Shrugged and mumbled when asked a question.

Classmates called him a loner.

His throat tightened and he stammered; the girl laughed at him and told him not to talk to her.

He nodded a thank you when the principal handed him one of the last diplomas of the stack.

"Get out, and never talk to me again!" his father shouted, throwing the boy's clothes onto the wet driveway.

"Just shut up and do your work," his boss told him. "When I want your advice, I'll ask for it."

SILENCE IS GOLDEN.

He didn't approve of the war, but he never spoke out.

When the pretty girl at work came near, he turned away.

Two coworkers went hunting over a weekend and bragged about the deer they had killed. His eyes filled with tears as he looked down at his work.

The round soup spoon seemed too large for his mouth one evening when he was having his lonely dinner of canned soup heated on a hot plate.

The change dumped in his hand by the grocery clerk didn't add up to what he was due. He looked at the coins for a moment, and then walked away.

The rent for his small room was increased the second time in six months. He read the notice several times before putting the bills in an envelope and quietly sliding it under the landlord's door.

It was difficult for him to get a teaspoon in his mouth when he ate his soup that night.

He got a good look at the boy who knocked down the elderly lady and took her purse. He knew where the boy lived. He disappeared into the crowd that had gathered.

A customer was charged for work that had not been done. He silently watched as his boss grinned and stuffed the extra into his pocket.

On his way home he bought a box of straws so he could sip his warmed broth.

Someone remarked that he seemed to be getting thin, and asked if there was anything wrong. He shook his head.

A handful of people stood around the open casket. "He was very reserved." "I didn't really know him." "He looks so natural."

They stood quietly looking at him until the lid was closed.

Only one--a child--noticed that he had no mouth. "Look, mama," he started, "he doesn't have..."

Her mother squeezed her shoulder. "Hush, little baby. Hush

The Lighthouse

He watched the ocean as though searching for something lost at sea a long time before, his eyes narrow slits in a face lined from years of wind and salt air.

He stood tall and erect, his gnarled hands gripping the weathered iron railing around the catwalk at the top of the lighthouse. His white mustache and neatly trimmed beard were stained amber around his mouth from the pipe clenched between his teeth. The Captain's cap that he wore was pulled low on his forehead and a heavy, blue sea coat protected him from the chilling night wind.

The water glistened in never ending patterns and the round-leafed sea grapes formed silver edged dark clumps in the moonlight. The foam from the breakers glowed in the bright, bluish light as they rolled onto the wet sand of the beach.

Above and behind him, inside the round, glass room, the drive mechanism of the light hummed, barely audible, above the sound of the wind blowing off the ocean. Twice every minute the great light, magnified by the Fresnel lens, swept above his head, pointing its long, bright finger toward the horizon as though helping the man in his search.

Some miles away to the north, lights glowed intensely around a cluster of low, drab buildings and a single, tall tower.

The heavy metal door behind the man swung open and a man dressed in gray emerged from the interior of the lighthouse.

He greeted the one at the rail, "Good evening, Captain Williams, it's a beautiful night, ain't it?"

"Good evening, Sergeant Thompson. Yes, it is beautiful and no better place in the world to enjoy it than up here."

The two were silent for a few minutes as the Sergeant joined the Captain at the rail, standing not as close to the edge and gripping the rail tighter than the captain. Then the Captain spoke:

"I always wanted Martha to come up here on nights like this. She did a few times, but she said the wind mussed her hair and it was too far to the ground. Things like that bother women."

"Yes sir, I guess they do," the Sergeant replied," then added, "bother women," as he took one hand from the rail to hug his coat closer and pull his square-billed cap a little lower on his forehead. His other hand stayed in place, tightly gripping the rail.

"Your little Davey used to like to come up here with you," Sergeant Thompson continued. "Remember how he'd run up all those steps, 'round and 'round to beat you to the top? Then he'd stand up here when it seemed like the wind would likely blow him away and he'd just hang on and laugh."

Sergeant Thompson always talked too much, the Captain thought to himself. He didn't have to be reminded about Davey. He hadn't especially liked the sergeant when he and the other soldiers had been assigned to guard the lighthouse during the war, but he had become a close friend after Davey had been lost at sea. They had walked the beach together for days hunting for something ...anything. It wasn't right that a twelve year-old boy couldn't be buried beside his mother and grandmother under the oaks west of the lighthouse.

He could still picture the sloop as it broke up a half mile offshore in the winter storm. He could only stand where he now stood and watch helplessly as the sails tore away and the mast splintered and crashed into the churning, gray water. With control lost, the hull broached, waves thundered over the gunwale and the boat capsized.

Davey had been coming home for Christmas. He had been sent to St. Augustine to live with the Captain's brother after Martha had died of the fever. The Captain would visit four times a year when he made the overnight trip to St. Augustine to make his report and collect his pay. After Davey was old enough he would come back to the lighthouse as a free passenger on the supply boat and stay the summer when school was out and during Christmas holidays.

Davey had loved the lighthouse and the ocean, the green turtle steaks, the oranges and pineapples that grew behind the lighthouse keeper's house, and he loved to fish in the lagoon. Many times he had told his father that some day he would be grown and he would be the lighthouse keeper. But that was never to be.

"How long do you think it will be?" the Sergeant interrupted the Captain's thoughts, gesturing toward the lights.

Captain Williams looked to the north, "Shouldn't be long now, maybe ten, fifteen minutes. Lot's going on up there."

The Sergeant studied the lights, "Yep, reckon you're about right ...ten, fifteen minutes," he echoed.

"You know," the Sergeant continued, "I didn't like this place when I first got sent here. Thought it was the most God-forsaken place I'd ever seen. If the skeeters didn't eat you up, the rattlesnakes or the gators would get you. In the summer you'd think you were goin' to burn up completely and the sun would parch your skin. Then, in the winter, that wind would blow off the ocean an' cut plumb through you. I been colder here than I been up in Kentucky. But there's days and nights that are so good you don't never want them to end. After a while you get that old sand in your shoes and you don't want to leave, and if you do, you'll come back, like I did.

Captain Williams continued his searching of the sea. "I've been here since '42," he said. I got the job of lighthouse keeper in '47. Been a lot of changes out here since then. Lots of changes ...roads and buildings been built and..."

"Bears are gone and most of the deer," the Sergeant interrupted. "I don't know what they call some of those things they've built...strange looking things...big, tall buildings without no walls. Say, I can see what looks like smoke up there. Goin' to be soon now." He looked at the captain. "It's got to be soon if we're going to see it. The sun will be coming up in a few minutes."

Moments after he spoke, a brilliant, gold light spread from the area where the building and the lights were located, lighting the land and the sky. Seconds later there was a tongue of flame that began to rise into the sky, slowly at first, accelerating as it rose higher.

A low rumbling began and grew to an ear-shattering roar that made the lighthouse shake. As the flame climbed higher it began a slow arc across the sky, growing dimmer as it moved into the night. The roar faded into silence. A cloud-like trail lighted by the still hidden sun marked the path of the flaming object.

The two men standing at the top of the lighthouse watched the dot of light as it made its flight away from them, gradually becoming smaller and smaller until it disappeared into the darkness. The men stood, watching the sky silently, for minutes after the light had gone.

The Sergeant broke the silence, "The way that thing's goin', you'd think it was headed for the moon." He chuckled at the thought.

The captain stood silently, searching the waves. "I wish Davey could have seen that," he said softly, "I wish Davey ..." his voice faded.

"Guess we'd best go, Captain," Sergeant Thompson urged softly, looking at the man beside him, "Like I said, goin' to be daylight soon."

The Captain remained still, looking out to the sea. "I'd like to see the sun come up over the ocean just once more," he said softly.

"Yes sir, I would too, but we both know there ain't no way we can do that. We'd best go now."

The two made their way inside the lighthouse and down the steel, circular stairs that led to the ground level. They exited through the heavy steel door at the base and started to walk toward the row of giant oaks that stood to the west of the lighthouse.

Halfway to the trees, the Captain stopped and looked back toward the tall structure silhouetted against the soft glow building in the east.

"That one was most loud enough to wake the dead, wasn't it Captain?" the Sergeant asked, smiling.

Captain Williams looked at his friend and returned the smile, "You might say that, Sergeant, you just might say that."

The two old friends turned and walked slowly into the deep shadows of the oaks, toward the waiting granite stones with the chiseled inscriptions:

WILLIAM A. THOMPSON
Sergeant 39th Kentucky Inf. CSA
Born Feb. 3, 1840
Died May 16, 1908

CAPTAIN DAVID C. WILLIAMS, SR.
Lighthouse Keeper
Cape Canaveral Light
Born July 27, 1804
Died Oct. 21, 1889

T0 BE READ IN BLACK AND WHITE ONLY

I stood in the dense fog looking for her. Waiting for the last plane to leave--the last Piper Cub to Paduca.

"Play it again, Fred," I yelled over my shoulder to the Polynesian banjo picker working the smoke-filled honkey tonk behind me.

"You know I can't play that damned song," Fred shouted back at me.

Suddenly she was there, close in the dense fog before I could see her. Her, in that familiar broad-brimmed hat and that torn raincoat.

She pulled an envelope from the pocket of her raincoat.

A vial of sleeping pills fell to the flooded tarmac.

"This is for you. From the colonel," she said in her phony Swedish accent as she handed me the letter.

I looked down at the pills that rolled out of the vial and into the puddle at my feet.

"So you're the one," I said, "the one who made the colonel swallow the four hundred sleeping pills secreted in his tapioca. The one who persuaded him to eat your arsenic-laced bouillabaisse...your instant mashed potatoes loaded with strychnine."

A tear rolled down her cheek.

"Are you going to turn me in," she asked. "Does this mean that our days of working together as spies are over?"

"No," I replied. "I like your style. We'll be together in this thing until we beat them."

I chucked her under the chin.

"Here's cooking with you, kid."

I **NEVER** HAD A **DAUGHTER**

I never had a daughter
Pink blankets
Stuffed puppies and kittens
Tiny socks with lace
Little bow in baby hair
Dimpled cheeks
Dark brown hair
Like her mother...
But that would be nice.

I never had a daughter
Frilly dresses
Easter bonnets
Curly hair
Teasing eyes
Baby dolls
Tea sets
Playing house...
But that would be nice.

I never had a daughter
First dabs of makeup "
Hair in curlers
Special glances
The boy next door
Bikini too small
Shirt too large
Shopping for hours…
But that would be nice.

I never had a daughter
Special prom dress

Makeup just right
A special boy
Staying out too late
Love in her eyes
Diamond on her finger
Grown up and beautiful...
But that would be nice.

I never had a daughter
Showing her emotions
No fear, no shame
A great big hug
A kiss on the cheek
When she sees me
Dabbing at tears
When we part...
But that would be nice.

I never had a daughter
Just two fine sons
To make me proud
Grown now
Bigger than I
Too big for a hug
Or a kiss on the cheek
Or a few tears when we part…
But that would be nice.

Grandmother

This is not a short story I wrote, but I think it will be interesting to some readers. This is a letter written by my great grandmother to her sister announcing the birth of my grandmother. Some may look at the date of the letter—1858—and think that it should be about the birth of my great grandmother, but it is about my grandmother. My mother was adopted in 1907 by Anna and Charles Maddux when my mother was only two years old. When they adopted her grandmother was fifty years old and grandfather was sixty-one years old. They had no children of their own.

My maternal grandfather, William Wadford, died in his late twenties as a result of malaria and yellow fever contracted during his service in the Spanish American war, leaving grandmother with three young daughters. Grandfather was buried in a pauper's grave. My grandmother did not go to grandfather's funeral because she gave birth to my mother that day. There was no social security, army pension or other government program to help grandmother raise three daughters. The oldest daughter was sent to live with relatives in Maryland.

Charles and Anna Maddux saw my mother with her mother and her sister on the streets of St. Petersburg. The three were in tattered clothes. They took pity on them and offered some help. Shortly afterward they asked if they could adopt my mother, Edna. Grandmother, Grace Wadford, agreed and the paperwork was done. Charles and Anna Maddux were well off. He was a civil engineer and she was a realtor.

I have done no editing. Grammar and spelling errors are as they appear in the original letter. In one case I could not read a word from the faded brown ink on yellowed paper.

* * * *

Sept. 16th/1858

My dear Sister

As David has not finished his letter yet, I concluded to get another sheet for fear of not leaving him enough room. I will not attempt to give you any news at this time as I suppose David will give you the particulars. I only wish to tell you something about our sweet little babe. She was born the 2nd of August, has deep blue eyes, dark hair, nose like its Pa, forehead and mouth exactly like yours. Mother says it is a real little Mag. Oh! Mag it is so sweet and pretty I know you could scarcely keep from biting her, Don't write to any of us to kiss it for you, for it looks like they will eat the little thing up, Pa, David, Cliff and Shelton, I don't know which is worst, all have to nurse it a little while every night, and Sammy can't keep his hands off of it, and says if it ever goes to Ky. He "is going to." Oh! Mag she has the brightest eyes you ever saw. We can't decide on a name, one selects a name another says it is to ugly, and so it goes. Mother and David has one selected, but I don't like it very well, Annie Mariah is there selection. Mother don't want her called Margaret.

Sept. 18th. I stoped writing, went to the fair yesterday. Saw everybody most. I saw Dr. Henderson and Chalmers, Cousin Ester, Cousin Bettie, Cousin Nan D., Cousin Sam, May and Relo Vaughn, Dr. Bridgford, Eliza & Tom Dudly, Mr. Vansennger, Arch, Van and almost everybody else, Cousin Nannie Hagan was there but I did not see her. John Burke took a premium on his fine saddle mare. I don't think Dick has been to see Nan for some time. Arch took her to the association in a buggy. Some think they will marry. We are going to see Cousin Adelia soon. I left the babe with Ma yesterday.

Cousin Bettie had her babe out and called to David to know if his was as pretty as hers. He blushed and said yes a great deal prettier. Arch has called on Kip Steele twice. What do you think about that? Cousin Georgia has a little daughter. Her Ma has been up to see her,

19th. Ma and Pa has gone to Paris to church. David, Clifton and Shelton to the schoolhouse, and I am old folks at home. Well Mag just one year ago yesterday you came here for the first time. Oh! What strange things can take place in one year. The babe is awake and I must stop and take her up.

22nd. I now attempt to close this. We had the Mike Smiths and Kip Vansennger to see us last night. Cousin Nan, De B. and Mary U. has promised me a visit this week. Dear Sister you must write to us soon, write a long letter. Give my love to Pa, Ma and Atlas. Mother sends her love. Cliff talks often of writing to you. Sammy says he would like to see you but he don't want you to come here for he fears you would take the baby. I will not ask you to excuse this, just xxxx it if you can.

Your affectionate sister

    Lucy McC..Steele

• * * * *

The name they agreed on was Anna Mariah Gosney. Grandmother's Uncle, Shelton Gosney, was killed in 1861 during the "Battle of the Bales" outside Lexington Missouri. His body was taken home in a horse-drawn buggy. In his pocket were a twist of tobacco wrapped in brown paper and a red silk bandana. We have both of them stored in plastic. After 154 years the sniff test assures you that it is tobacco wrapped in brown paper.

Parade

FAR DOWN THE WAY
COOL, EARTHY TONES OF
FLUTES AND CLARINETS
SWELLING WITH THE WARMTH OF
SAXOPHONES, ALTO, TENOR, BARITONE
THE STRENGTH OF BRASS
TRUMPETS
TROMBONES
THUNDER OF DRUMS
CRASH OF CYMBALS
THE UM PA PA
OF BASSES
FADING INTO
THE DISTANCE.
THE ONLY
BAND
IN THE

30

THE MAN IN GRAY

Every other Friday I go straight to the bank after work to cash my pay check, deposit most of it and get some cash to carry me two weeks to the next pay day. I hoped there wouldn't be cops between work and the bank today. I had to work late and needed to make it to the bank before it closed.

I wheeled into the bank parking lot with only seconds to spare. There was one other car in the lot, an old Ford with bad complexion and a splatter of rust freckles. I assumed the small man dressed in oily gray lounging against the wall near the door was its owner.

The guard took his finger off the button that lowered the steel security panels that covered the front windows and doors. The panels stopped half way down so I had to stoop to get through the door.

"Cut it pretty close this time," the guard said with a grin. "Saw you jump out of your car and run toward the door so I held up for you.

As I bent down to get under the security panels I felt a hand on my back pushing me forward. "Hurry," a hoarse voice said. "Keep moving. Go-go-go." A quick look over my shoulder told me it was the man in gray.

"Hey," the guard yelled, "You can't get in here like that!"

"Screw you," the man in gray yelled back, "I'm in, ain't I? Just like I planned." He punched the guard who fell backward and hit his head on the tile floor

As I started to straighten up, the man in gray gave me a hard shove with a gloved hand. I fell forward and landed on my hands and knees. He gave me another shove. This time with a dirty Nike on the seat of my jeans. "Crawl over there and turn around and face me." He pulled a couple of grocery store plastic bags from his back pocket, wadded them and threw them to the tellers. "Fill them up and don't push no buttons back there. Just fill them bags."

The elderly guard wobbled to his feet and started fumbling with the holster hanging on his right side. As he pulled out his ancient small-caliber revolver, the man in gray pulled a cheap six-shooter from the hand warmer pocket on the front of his hoodie and fired one shot. The guard fell again, holding his side. The man in gray took a couple of steps, scooped up the guard's gun, and stuck it in his hip pocket. "Just like I planned. Figured he would go for his gun." He reached in his hand warmer again, pulled out another cheap pistol, fumbled with the two guns for a few seconds and then bent down and slid one across the floor. It stopped close to my feet. "Pick it up."

"What?"

"I said pick it up. Don't mess up my plan. That pistol had only one round in it. I used that one on that ol' man they call a guard. I said for you to pick it up. Do it."

I did as he said.

The man in gray smiled. "Now there ain't nobody's finger prints on that gun 'cept yours. I wore these gloves so my prints ain't on it...just like I planned."

He looked toward the ladies behind the counter, "Fill them bags." Still holding his pistol pointed at me, he glanced at his watch. "I gave myself five minutes in here and I'm running close." He turned back toward me, "If you don't think that is empty, point it at me...right here" the man in gray patted his sweat shirt above the hand warmer. "That gun is empty. Point it here. Right here. I want your fingerprints all over that gun. The police will be sure that you shot the guard. Now, pull the trigger! Do it!"

I did as he said.

The man in gray looked down at the red spot growing on his sweatshirt.

He looked at the gun still in his hand, moaned as he dropped to his knees. "Wrong damned gun," he said as he slid face down onto the floor. "I didn't plan that."

Sticks

Coley Martin heard the tapping and whapping while the boy was still a block away. There wasn't any rhythm to the tapping, just "tappin' and whappin" as Coley called it, the sound of some kid with a new pair of drumsticks that he didn't know how to use...just tapping and whapping away at everything, anything, beating those sticks to pieces on the concrete sidewalk, on brick walls, on fences, garbage cans, anything that made a noise. Coley knew that anything became a drum to the ears of a kid with a new pair of drumsticks that he didn't know how to use.

By the time he got close, where Coley could see him, the kid had stopped "tappin' and whappin '" on everything and was walking along the sidewalk humming and clacking the sticks together... sort of in time with his steps.

"Say, boy, what you got there?" Coley said in a deep, booming voice that seemed to come from somewhere far down in his three-hundred pound frame... a voice that seemed to shout, no matter what Coley said or how he said it. The boy stopped and looked up at the shiny black face with its close cropped white hair, and the body that spread halfway across the front steps of the apartment building. The big man's shirt was frayed about the collar, but was starched and ironed with sharp, precise creases. His black trousers were shiny in spots, but they too were neatly pressed.

Coley lifted his chin from his hands crossed on the top of the cane, the tip rested on a lower step between his feet ...huge feet cozied into bright red socks--Coley Martin's trademark--and pushed partway into soft bedroom slippers. He looked at the kid who looked like any of the hundreds of boys who lived within a few blocks in the city, a scrawny kid wearing jeans and bulky high-top basketball shoes, a tee shirt too large for skinny shoulders and a cap turned so the bill shaded the back of his neck.

"Boy, I say what you got there?" Coley said again to the kid who stood and looked in silence at this behemoth with the thundering voice.

"Drum sticks," the boy finally managed.

"Where you get them drum sticks, boy?"

"I give a dollar for them to a boy I know."

"You a drummer?"

"Not yet, but I gonna be."

"Come 'ere. Come on up here an' let me see them sticks. Come on, I ain't gonna bite." Coley's mouth opened into a wide, toothy grin that showed a gold sparkle in front.

The boy came partway up the steps and stretched his arm out, holding the ends of the sticks, the other ends pointed toward Coley. Coley took the sticks in one hand, held them up and twisted and turned them, weighing them, evaluating them. He took a stick in each hand in the traditional drummer's grip...left hand palm up, the stick under the thumb, little finger and ring finger bent with the stick resting on them, the other two fingers curled over the stick...right hand palm down, stick between the thumb and forefinger...sticks held loosely, not in the two-fisted, clubbing grip of the rock drummers.

The kid watched Coley's moves with the sticks. "You a drummer?" the kid asked.

"Well, yeah...I used to be. You say you gonna be a drummer, huh? You know anything about drummin', boy? How you gonna learn to be a drummer? Somebody gonna teach you? First thing you got to learn is that you don't go 'round tappin' an' whappin' on the sidewalk or buildings, stuff like that. Tears up them sticks. Don't practice on nothin' but a rubber practice pad, or a piece of smooth wood if you ain't got a practice pad."

"I'm gonna watch TV an' music videos an' do what them drummers do. I can learn. I'm gonna watch them and do what they do an' when I can, I'm gonna buy me a big, shiny set of drums an' get me a job playing with one of them big bands on TV. Wham! Bang bang, boom," the kid flayed his arms around in the air copying the motions of a wild drummer.

Coley held his forearm up as a mock shield against the flapping arms of the kid and smiled. "Look out now, you gonna break all them drum heads the first time you play on them if you beat on them like that." He switched the sticks back and forth, hand to hand, testing the feel of each one. "Boy," he said, "do you know which one of these sticks is the right hand stick and which one is the left hand stick?"

"They both the same...ain't they?"

"The same? No, boy the right stick comes from the right side of the tree and the left stick comes from the left side of the tree." Coley lowered his head and looked at the boy with the stern expression of a teacher who had just made a profound statement.

The kid looked at Coley with an expression that said he wasn't sure that what he was hearing was the truth. His eyes were wide and searching as he looked at the big man.

Coley gave the kid a light poke in the stomach with the sticks, opened his mouth wide and rolled out a bass laugh. "Ho, boy, I jus' joshin' with you. It don't matter what side of the tree they came from. What I mean is that you have to feel the sticks...play with them a little bit to get the feel of them so you know which one is for your right hand and which one is for left hand. Here, take them, one in each hand and close your eyes. Tell me which one is heavier-switch them back an' forth 'tween your hands till you can tell me which one is heavier."

The kid followed Coley's instructions, squinching his eyes shut and switching the sticks back and forth.

"This one," he said after a minute, "I think this one is heavier."

"That's good, That's real good!" Coley praised. "If you right handed, that heavy one is for your left hand. Your right hand is a little stronger so you naturally hit a little harder with that hand, so you use the heavy one in your left hand to make up for it. Otherwise, when you play right, left, right, left, it'll sound like bap, bip, bap, bip, instead of bap, bap, bap, bap. Want them taps--that's what them little hits are called--to sound just alike. Look, that one got a dark spot on the shaft so that's the one you use in your left hand. Now here's how you hold them." He showed the kid, first holding them himself and then arranging them in the boy's hands.

"Now, you move them sticks like this," he motioned with his hands. "It's all in the wrists. You learn first to use your wrists and let the sticks do the work, then you can learn some of that loud, fancy stuff. Right now, you got to learn taps an' strokes, flams, ruffs, drags, long roll, short rolls, ratemacues, paradiddles, double paradiddles..."

"What? What's all them things? I never heard of any of them things!"

"They're called rudiments. You gotta learn them first." Coley thought a second, looking at the kid's pained expression. "An' you got to teach them sticks by startin' off real slow and then, when it starts gettin' easy, you start gettin' faster an' faster. But them sticks don't know nothin' when you first get them, so you got to take your time an' teach them right. You learn an' you teach them sticks at the same time."

Coley maneuvered his body around and took the kid's small hands in his big paws, with the kid holding the sticks the way Coley had shown him. "Start slow an' easy, like this. Tap with the left, then with the right, see? Tap, tap, left, right, left, right, tap, tap. Nice an' loose, tap, tap, left, right. That's good, that's good."

"What grade you in, boy?" Coley asked as he shifted back to his previous position on the steps.

"Six grade. I'm twelve."

"You like school? You doin' OK?"

"Not very good. I don't like school. I'm just goin' til I can play drums good enough to get me a job an' then I'm goin' to quit."

Coley frowned at the boy's words. "Can't do that," he said. "MM MMM, can't do that. You need to go to school and learn all you can to be a good drummer and get a job in a big band."

"What kind of things I need to learn?"

Coley thought a second. "Math. You like math?"

"I hate math. Why do I have to learn math to be a drummer?"

"Fractions," Coley said. "You got to know about fractions so you can understand about half notes and quarter notes and eighth notes and sixteenth, and all that. Drummin' ain't nothin' but math...dividin' up measures of music into fractions...the more beats, the more fractions. When you get to learning to read music you'll understand why you got to learn fractions, math.

"Geography," Coley continued, "You got to know geography, too."

"What for?"

"Why, boy, if somebody says you got to play in Boston this week an' Chicago next week an' then you got to to London or Australia, you got to know where those places are, and how to get there, and what you can see and do when you get there. Got to know geography. An' English. You doin' good in English class?"

The kid shook his head.

Coley understood the boy's feelings. He had dropped out of school but had been lucky enough to find steady work as a drummer. He had been good, had taken lessons and learned the rudiments, how to play the right way. He had made enough to marry Irene and to raise a couple of children and put them through college, but things had been different back then. Got to get an education today.

"Hmmm, English is mighty important. You talk bad English an' folks think you not very smart. You get to be a big time drummer and folks from television and magazines gonna want to interview you an' write all about you, an' you gotta be able to talk right. Yeah, English is mighty important. Everything you get in school is mighty important. You got to work hard to learn all the things you need to know to be a good drummer. You ready to do that, boy?"

The kid looked down at the steps. He was still holding the drum sticks the way Coley had shown him. He nodded his head. "Yessir.'

Coley leaned his cane against his leg. He reached out to the kid and put one hand on each of the boy's skinny shoulders. "Look at me, boy," he said in a soft rumble. "Tell you what I'll do. You work hard in school and you learn as much as you can, an' I'll teach you to be a drummer. Long as you get good grades, I'll teach you. Let's see, this is Wednesday. You come by here every Wednesday after school and bring those sticks. You tell me what you learned in school, and I'll teach you drummin'. You do your school homework and you practice what I teach you and one of these days you gonna be a drummer. I'll teach you as long as you stay in school. An' I want to see your report cards. I want to make sure you learnin' all those things you need to know to be a good drummer." Coley smiled and showed the gold sparkle. OK?"

"OK."

"Good. You go along now an' I'll see you next Wednesday afternoon. I'll be out here on these steps an' I'll bring a practice pad. You gonna learn right out here where everybody can see you so they can see you doin' somethin' important. Make it easier the first time you got to play in front of a crowd, too. I'll see you next Wednesday."

The kid ran down the street, still holding the drum sticks the way Coley had shown him.

Coley raised himself off the step, using his cane and the balustrade to help lift his bulk. He moved slowly, on stubborn legs that didn't want to do as they were directed. He opened the door to his first-floor apartment and stepped into a clean, neat living room decorated with dozens of framed photographs of bandleaders and other celebrities with a younger, trimmer Coley Martin behind a set of white, pearl-finish drums. In one corner of the room was the same set of drums, the white pearl finish yellowed and the brass cymbals tarnished from the years.

Irene looked up from the crossword puzzle she was working. Coley was standing by the drums. He tapped a finger tip on one of the cymbals.

"Who was that you were talking to out there, Cole?" Irene asked.

"Just a kid. Just some kid that came along tappin' and whappin' with a pair of drum sticks."

"Were you talking to him about learning to play drums?"

"No... No, I was talkin' to him about stayin' in school."

The Smell of Pine

A frontier home
A pioneer family
A baby boy
Wrapped in homespun blankets
Tenderly placed in a handmade cradle—
His first smell of pine

A little boy's toy boat
Bobbing down a rocky stream
A stick for a mast
Paper for a sail
Hull carved from a plank—
The fresh smell of pine

Snow on the hillside
Stockings filled with gifts
Fresh game for dinner
Christmas songs sung
To the strum of a guitar
Simple presents under a decorated tree—
The joyful smell of pine

A small, white chapel filled
With pump organ's sweet, practiced notes
A smiling young groom beside
A beautiful bride in hand-stitched white
Loved ones seated in hand-carved pews—
The sacred smell of pine

A homestead farm
A new home
Of fresh hewn logs.
Cattle grazing within a
Barbed wire fence stretched

Between fresh cut posts—
The secure smell of pine

A dispute of rights
Words said in anger
A threat to life
Barbed wire ripped and twisted
From broken posts—
The acrid smell of pine

A confrontation in the forest
Threatening words
Guns drawn in anger
A single shot echoing through the hills
A young man lying on a gray-green carpet—
The musty smell of pine

A grave dug in rocky ground
A plain wooden coffin
The mourning bride weeping
The young man's body
in cheap undertaker's black
Handsome face covered close by a wooden lid—
His last smell of pine.

Ella Jean

1936

Ella Jean leaned against the side of the small building that housed the restrooms behind the two-story frame school and watched the men chop into pieces the big tree that had been struck by lightning during summer vacation. She was a good distance from them, but the smell of sweat, dirt and tobacco overpowered the aroma of the fresh cut oak. They were mostly black, but there were four white men. Some of the men had stripped off their black and white striped shirts.

Their bodies were shiny wet with sweat from the heat of the early September Florida sun. Most of the men wore work-stained hats. They all wore pants with broad black and dirty white stripes, heavy work shoes and chain shackles locked between their ankles. Their work was slow paced but steady. One of the white men turned and looked at Ella Jean for a time. His face was blank, then his eyes softened and the corners of his mouth moved up a little as he looked at her. He turned away and went back to chopping a big limb.

The man in dirty khaki spat a stream of brown liquid, shifted the shotgun cradled in his arms and walked slowly toward Ella Jean. On the front of a belt loosely slung below his big belly was a brown leather holster with a small caliber revolver pointing down toward his crotch.

"Hey, young'un, you bes' git back over on the other side of the toilet house an' play with them other kids," the man in khaki said in a loud voice as he walked toward Ella Jean. "Go on now, git away from here."

Ella Jean looked at the man's sparse brown teeth. He doesn't practice good dental hygiene, she thought, Mrs. Barber taught us about that last year in the second grade.

"Ella Jean, what are you doing around here? I said you could go to the bathroom, but I didn't say you could stand around here and gawk at these prisoners. They're bad men.

They've done terrible things and you shouldn't be near them." Mrs. Carpenter stood with her fists digging into her skinny hips and looked at Ella Jean and then at the men. "Young lady, you just get yourself around to the other side and play dodge ball with the others. Recess is almost over." She gave Ella Jean a push with the back of her hand and followed her to where the others were playing.

The bell rang and the children formed two lines, girls in one, boys in the other. As they filed into the building she heard one of the boys whisper to another, "How many people you think they killed? All them murdered somebody, that's why they're wearin' them chains on their legs."

Ella Jean's desk was next to the big windows that opened top and bottom to provide ventilation in the high-ceilinged classroom that smelled of old varnish, mopped wood floors, chalk, crayons and the contents of twenty odd lunch boxes and greasy paper sacks. She could hear the axes slamming into the remains of the big oak. Whenever Mrs. Carpenter turned her back to write on one of the big blackboards that covered most of two walls, Ella Jean would rise up in her seat and look out at the men in black and white.

Mrs. Carpenter turned from writing something about Columbus and 1492 just as a saliva-soaked wad of chewed paper sailed across the room and hit Rose White, leaving a dark spot on the shoulder of her blue dress.

The scrawny little teacher marched straight to Frank Whaley, lifted him from the wood desk seat with one hand and whapped him hard and fast five times with a well worn ruler before Frank could lie that he, "...ain't done nothin'," took him by the ear and led him stumbling and squawking to the front of the room, drew a circle on the blackboard about Frank's eye level, pushed his nose into the center of the circle and told him to keep it there, all the while scolding Frank and all the other boys who would-surely-be-the-death-of-her-one-day, that they were all going to end up in prison stripes like those they had seen outside at recess if they didn't change their ways. "They have all done terrible things," she said in a loud voice. "They are bad people. Some of them will be in prison for ten or twenty years because of the bad things they did. Can any of you imagine what it would be like to be in prison and not even see your family for twenty years...from now until nineteen fifty-six?"

* * * *

Ella Jean sat doing her homework at the kitchen table in the little, weather-faded yellow house on Tenth Street and watched her mother stir the contents of a pot simmering on the kerosene stove.

"Mama, what are we having for supper," Ella Jean asked.

"Fish, grits and pork-and-beans."

"We have that a lot."

"Lucky we have that. Little bit of relief money we get don't buy much. Dooley Cass dropped by to give us some bream he caught. The beans don't cost much, and a bag of grits goes a long way."

Ella Jean's mother turned the fish that sizzled in an iron skillet. "What did you do at school today, Honey?"

Ella Jean crossed her arms atop the book she had been reading. She rested her chin on her arms and stared blankly toward the screen door across the room.

"I saw Daddy."

The Movement of Life

Feet ever moving
arms ever reaching
hands grasping at nothing
a voice without words
body bathed by another's
loving hands
tears of joy
the softness of sleep
the joy of birth.

Steps unsure, hesitant
hands grasping for support
from things nearby
for a helping hand
to steady faltering steps.

Dashing, darting,
climbing, running, ,
moving, jumping
searching for new adventures
exploring new places
waking to sleeping.

Walk slowly to the music
proudly down the aisle
caps and gowns
reach for the diploma
shake the hand
knowledge gained
to be forgotten.

Jaunty gait,

lively steps ready to meet challenges
of the world
confidence to meet life
promises of the future.

Hup two, hup two,
keep in step
over hard, hot pavement
freezing snow, slipping sand,
steaming jungle
forward at the command
forward to kill
forward to die

Walk slowly to the music
muffled drums
flag-draped coffin
a lonely bugle
the crack of rifles
a fallen comrade
a lost friend.

Walk slowly to the music
down the aisle
soft organ tones
sweet blossoms' aroma
a gown of white
promises made
a band of gold
a shower of rice
run to the waiting carriage.

Pacing, pacing to and fro
waiting, waiting
for a word
pacing, pacing to and fro

a nurse in white
the awaited words
a cry
a child.

Walk slowly
hand extended
a hand helping
steadying the first steps
hands full of help
heart full of love.

Strong steps
confident pace
steady steps of security
to work
to home
to work
to home
to work
to home

Steps heavy with drudgery
steps heavy with boredom
the sameness of work
the sameness of life
steps heavy with doubt
of self
of past
of future.

Steps slowed
by the press of years
slowly pacing
a stop for breath
aimless steps of loneliness

when one so long loved
is gone.

Steps unsure, hesitant
grasping for support
from things nearby
for a helping hand
to steady
faltering steps.

Feet ever moving
arms ever reaching
hands grasping at nothing
a voice without words
body bathed by another's
loving hands
tears of sadness
the softness of sleep
the stillness of death

WAITING

Early every morning the elderly woman walked a mile down the two-rut sand road, another half mile on the old, rough "hard road" and then disappeared into brush and palmetto covered acreage. On this crisp Florida morning she wore an old black coat, her hands crossed to hold it tight, a battered purse grasped in one hand and a stained paper sack in the other. Her white hair contrasted with the black coat. Her shuffling gait and rounded shoulders attested to her age.

There were no houses or businesses near the junction of the two roads, just the decaying remnants of a gas station and a general store that once served a small settlement and a decrepit railroad depot where trains never came.

****

A dark sedan with magnetic signs on the doors indicating the vehicle belonged to the largest realty firm in the nearby town pulled over to the side of the road. The driver and passenger got out and the driver addressed the other, "This is the parcel of land I told you about, Mr. Baker. I think it would be ideal for your warehouse. Twenty acres. Nice and flat."

"Let's walk around out there. Want to see if it's all flat like this—no surprises."

They had tramped through the brush for a few minutes when Baker pointed. "What's that? Looks like a roof."

The realtor looked where Baker was pointing. "That's what's left of the old depot. Train used to come through here. Closed it down, took out the rails years ago. It's not on this property."

Baker pushed aside limbs of a tall bush. "I'd like to take a look. I've always been interested in old railroads."

They waded through the underbrush until they reached the edge of a cracked, weed-ridden concrete deck. They stopped and looked at each other. Across the concrete slab an elderly little woman in a black coat sat on the remains of an ancient bench.

Baker spoke first. Ma'am are you alright?"

The woman tuned slowly and looked at the men.

"Are you alright?" Baker repeated.

"Yes."

"What are you doing here all by yourself?"

"Waiting."

"Waiting? Waiting for what?" the second man asked.

The woman cupped her hand behind her ear. "What?"

The man spoke louder. "Waiting for what?"

"Waiting. Waiting for my brother." She paused, "Waiting for my brother to come home."

"Is he going to meet you here?"

"Yes. My older brother This is where he left; this is where he'll come home."

"He left here on the train?" Baker asked.

"Yes."

"Has he been gone a long time?"

"Yes…………a long time."

"Why did he leave?"

"He had to," she hesitated. "He…he was a marine…so handsome in his dress uniform…so handsome."

Baker asked, "When did he leave?"

The lady studied his question. "A long time ago. I was just a girl…thirteen years old when he left. He was a marine so he had to leave."

"Ma'am," the second man asked, "do you mind my asking how old you are now?"

"I'm getting old…not a girl anymore. I'm eighty-four…no, eighty-five."

The second man calculated on his fingers. "Nineteen forty-three. He left in nineteen forty-three?"

"….Yes, I think you're right. Nineteen forty-three."

"And you are still waiting?"

"Yes. Waiting. The last letter we got said he would be coming home soon…and then we got a box with his personal things in it. Should be home any day now. Morning train or evening train."

Baker stepped close and knelt in front of the lady. "Ma'am can we drive you home? Looks like it might rain soon."

"No, but thank you. The train should be here any time now and I don't want to leave before it comes. My brother will probably be on it. I'll be here, waiting. I'll stay here waiting until the train comes. Then I'll go home."

Baker stood up and looked at the other man. "I hate to leave her, but she's determined to stay." He looked at his watch. "Damn, it's later than I thought. I don't want to miss my flight home."

As they neared the car, both men stopped. They looked at each other.

"Did you hear that?" Baker half whispered.

The second man nodded slowly, "Sounded like the whistle of an old steam locomotive…in the distance."

Baker hesitated, "She will be there….."

The second man finished:

"Waiting."

Between Abelard and Zola

It was nearly midnight before we stopped to eat the cold sandwiches and the tepid tea that my sister Judith had brought along in a wicker basket. We ate quickly and with little conversation. Judith, our cousin Florence, and I had spent nearly twelve hours searching the rooms of our late Grandfather's old three-story mansion for what he had described in a letter as the key to his riches. Most of those hours had been spent in one room, his library. We had only twelve more hours to find what had been hidden. If we were unsuccessful, our claim to his fortune would be lost forever.

The books on the crowded shelves were warmed by the yellow glow from the coal oil lamps used to light the room. We had no need for the heat given off by the lamps. The room was without windows and the air was close. The room had been locked for nearly twenty years.

But perhaps it would be best if I started from the very beginning.

It was 1890 that Grandfather's Attorney, Mr. Julius Herkheimer, had read a letter from Grandfather, addressed to us, his grandchildren, that had been attached to Grandmother's will:

"You will find the key to my wealth is with what little remains of me. Through the simple application of the principles of logic one of you--or more than one should you decide to work as a team--will find the key to valuables worth a tidy sum, and guidelines that I have written to help you retain this bit of wealth and make it grow to great riches:

Reverend Lombard said it at my funeral.
Between Abelard and Zola.
All information is valuable. This is information.
Therefore, this information is valuable.

Aristotle, syllogism, premises, conclusions, deductive logic, inductive logic, symbolic logic.

Webster defines logic: 'The science that deals with the canons and criteria of thought and demonstration; the science of the formal principles of reason.'

Each of you, or each team, will have twenty-four hours to study my words, apply whatever degree of logic you may muster, and find the key to my wealth.

The eldest shall have the first twenty-four hours, the next eldest the second twenty-four, etc. I believe that this arrangement is fair. While the eldest may stumble on the treasure immediately, the others will have more time to use logic and to think. The first twenty-four hour period begins one hour from the time this letter is read to you."

Grandfather Thompson had died nearly twenty years before Grandmother. He had bequeathed some stocks and bonds and personal items to his children, my father and my father's brother, Uncle George, both now expired. In his will, he had stated that the remainder of his holdings would be distributed to his grandchildren in accordance with instructions to be revealed after grandmother had gone on to follow him.

The four grandchildren...my cousins, Conrad and Florence, my sister Judith and I...had just been read the part of Grandfather's will that made conditional distribution of the old three-story mansion on Fort King Road and all the other possessions he had left behind. The finder, or finders, of whatever we were to find would gain his remaining wealth.

We could have all worked together and shared equally, but Conrad, being the eldest, would have none of that. I had detected a certain degree of greediness when he had laughed and stamped his feet there in the office of Mr. Herkheimer, and said in a voice loud enough to be overheard in the bank below us on the first floor, "Hah! At last I will get what was rightfully mine twenty years ago!"

His younger sister, Florence, a lovely twenty-year-old who had never seemed overly bright, looked at Conrad with an expression that indicated surprise at Conrad's outburst and a lack of understanding of the significance of the whole thing. She asked Conrad if she could go with him, because she wouldn't know where to start, and was rather frightened at the thought of taking on such a mission on her own.

Cousin Conrad laughed and waved his cigar. "A fine lot of help you would be," he said. "I prefer to work alone, without the hindrance of any of you. I believe that I was Grandfather's favorite and that is the reason he stipulated that the eldest should have the first opportunity to find his riches. I shall be the owner of that great mansion and the finest carriage and team of horses in the city within the week. I may tolerate an occasional visit by the rest of you and I might--if I should see any one of you walking to your humble dwelling in a driving rain--offer you a ride in my carriage...or perhaps not. You might get my fine lap robe wet." He took a mighty draw from his cigar, blew out a cloud of malodorous smoke and laughed.

Mr Herkheimer cleared his throat and spoke in a soft voice. "I must give you a few rules that were not included in your Grandfather's letter. First, if you enter the house, nothing may be disturbed. If you pick up anything, you must put it back in place exactly as you found it. I must accompany you to insure that this rule is followed explicitly. You must understand the fairness of this rule. Nothing may be done that will hinder, in any way, the search of the others. Second, you must fully terminate your search precisely twenty-four hours after you begin. Third, you must stay at least three blocks away from the mansion until your time starts. Lastly, if none of you finds what you are looking for, the house, its contents and all other of your grandfather's possessions will be used to establish the Jeremiah Thompson Home for Unwed Mothers and Orphaned Children.

"By the way," he continued, "it is not to worry. Your Grandfather paid me in advance for my services--paid me well, I might add--so you do not have to concern yourselves over any fee being due from your inheritance. I wish each of you the best of luck."

Mr. Herkheimer rolled his high-backed chair to the corner of the room and twisted the tumbler on his office safe, carefully blocking our view of his manipulations with his rather corpulent backside, and locked Grandfather's and Grandmother's papers inside. He rolled back to his ornate mahogany desk, interweaved his fingers on top of his blotter pad and looked at the four of us. "I am at your service," he announced.

Cousin Conrad retrieved his bowler and cane from the floor beside his chair and jumped to his feet. "Then let us go," he shouted at Mr. Herkheimer, "I am ready. Get to your feet man."

Lawyer Herkheimer remained seated. His expression and his voice were calm. "Mr. Thompson," he said, "an hour remains before your time begins and this office is exactly three blocks from the mansion. You may go no closer until one hour from now--and do not make the mistake of going closer in the interim. If you do so, you will immediately forfeit claim to any part of your Grandfather's estate."

While Cousin Conrad grumbled, Judith and I gathered in the back of the office to discuss our strategy. Judith and I have always been close--probably because we are only eighteen months apart in age--so there was no hesitation on the part of either of us in deciding that we would work together as a team. Florence remained where she had been seated and looked about the dimly lighted office at the various certificates and engravings that lined the walls.

"Whatever shall we do about Florence?" Judith whispered. "She is the youngest, so she will be the last to try to find whatever it is that we are supposed to find. I'm not sure she could handle it by herself."

I looked at Florence. Her innocent, detached expression told me that what Judith had said was true. I had always liked Florence, but I had never cared for Conrad. He was boorish, and had been even more so when we were young. While I doubt that he had ever struck Florence, his bullying, domineering manner had frequently reduced her to tears and was, I believe, to a great degree responsible for her being such a shy, retiring person.

I stepped to Florence's chair and placed my hand lightly on her shoulder. She looked up at me and smiled. "Hello, John," she said as though seeing me for the first time that day, and patted my hand.

"Florence," I said, "Judith and I wondered if you would like to become a part of a team with us. If we find Grandfather's treasure, we will divide it in equal shares."

Her face brightened into a broad smile. "Oh, John, I would love to join with you and Judith. I'm afraid I wouldn't know where to begin if I was alone." She got up and, together, we walked to the corner of the room where Judith waited. Florence gave Judith a hug and said she was glad that we were going to work together.

We announced our intention to work as a team to Cousin Conrad and Lawyer Herkheimer. We thanked Mr. Herkheimer and left the office, closing the heavy door with its gold leaf lettering behind us. We went down the broad marble steps with the sturdy, carved balustrade and left the building through the door next to The City National Bank-- Grandfather's bank. He had built it from a small venture to a thriving enterprise with millions of dollars in assets.

My father and Conrad's father had worked at the bank, but had never risen to the position of President, the position in which Grandfather had served for many years. I had wondered about the status of the bank and its future. No one had been permanently appointed to that position since Grandfather's death. There had been only "caretakers" in the interim.

The three of us walked to the modest home that Judith and I shared with our widowed mother. Judith, a lovely young lady of twenty-four, had been pursued by several eligible young gentlemen, but she, feeling an obligation to our mother who was in poor health, had declined each suitor and chosen to care for mother for as long as she was needed. I, also feeling an obligation to our mother and responsibility for her mounting medical bills, had chosen to remain content with the life of a bachelor, so had worked with diligence in my position at Meyer's Emporium where I had risen from clerk to the position of assistant bookkeeper.

On the way to our home, I had stopped and talked with Mr. Meyer who had been kind enough to advance me two days of my one week annual vacation (without pay, of course) so that I could carry out the search for Grandfather's bequest.

After Judith made tea and brought cookies, the three of us sat in the parlor. We discussed what we had heard and what we had retained from our meeting at Mr. Herkheimer's office. None of us understood some of the references in Grandfather's letter. I knew that Abelard was an author, but neither Judith nor I was familiar with his works and we had no idea who Zola might be.

Poor Florence had little to share and spent most of the time walking about the room studying the porcelain statuettes that mother had collected over the years and the framed aquatint floral renderings that hung on the walls and, in one instance, the pattern of the wall paper.

"Do you think we should go to the cemetery first?" I asked Judith. "I believe Grandfather's message said something about the key to his wealth being with what little of him remains. Perhaps there would be something there."

"I suppose that would be a good place to ..."

"Grandfather was created," Florence interrupted as she studied a framed aquatint of a spray of violets.

I was surprised by her statement. "I beg your pardon?"

"Grandfather was created," she repeated, still studying the violets. "Conrad said he was created--all burned up."

"He was created? Do you mean he was cremated?" I asked.

Florence turned and looked at me and smiled. She rolled her eyes toward the ceiling and put a finger to her cheek. "Mmmmm," she hummed, "Maybe that was it, maybe that's what he said." She turned back to the violets.

I thought back. I had been very young when Grandfather had died and remembered little of his funeral. Judith had been even younger, and Florence, only a babe in arms. I did remember someone saying something that I hadn't understood at the time about Grandfather's ashes. Then I remembered that the headstone read: "In Memory of..." so Grandfather had been cremated. But where were his ashes? They had to be somewhere in the mansion on Fort King Road. I had visited Grandmother only a few times in the last several years, and knew little of most of the house. My more recent visits had been restricted to the formal parlor. I knew that Grandfather's ashes were not in that room. I would surely have noticed an urn of the type used for cremated remains.

Judith had been busily engaged in writing notes on what she had heard and what we had discussed since the meeting at Mr. Herkheimer's office. She adjusted the coal oil lamp on the writing table a trifle to provide better light, dipped her pen in the inkwell and made notes in flowing Spenserian script on a sheet of vellum. She paused to look at the paper.

"Grandfather had a study...or a library," she said suddenly, "just off the dining room. I remember once, when I was very young, I tried to open the door. Grandmother took my hand and led me away. She said that it had been Grandfather's room and that she had to keep the door locked.

Oh, Goodness, I remember, too, her saying that someday I would be permitted in that room...sometime in the future!"

"That's it!" I exclaimed," That's where his ashes must be, along with whatever we are to find. By the devil...oh. forgive me, I apologize for my uncouth outburst.

"We'll quickly look through the other rooms first, but if I were a wagering man I would be tempted to bet that we will find what we're hunting in that room!"

Florence had moved to a figurine of a Swiss girl. "What are we hunting?" she asked without turning to face us.

"I believe the words that Grandfather wrote said something about the key to his wealth being with what little remained of him," I answered. "What remains of him are ashes."

"If we find his ashes we might find a letter...or something," Judith said. "Or perhaps it's the other way around. Perhaps we must find a letter or a note...or maybe a notation in a book that will give us a clue to the location of Grandfather's ashes."

We talked for two hours. For the most part, Judith and I talked and Florence interjected an occasional irrelevant comment or asked a question that required little thought to answer. At four in the afternoon Florence bounced up from the chair where she had been seated for the past hour, after her sightseeing tour of the room. "Oh dear, I must go home. Mother will be worried if I am gone too long." She took her parasol from the umbrella stand and went to the door. I jumped to my feet and went to open the door and see her out.

"Now plan to be here at ten-thirty in the morning," I told Florence. "Conrad's twenty-four hours will be up at eleven and our's will start at twelve, so be here at ten-thirty. We should be at Mr. Herkheimer's office by eleven."

After supper, Judith had taken Mother's meal to her room and helped her arrange the tray on her bed. Judith washed the dishes and cleaned the kitchen while I continued my review of her notes. She joined me as soon as she completed her tasks. We talked and studied her notes, adding several that resulted from our discussion, until a late hour, and finally retired to our rooms after ten in the evening.

  I arose early, as was my habit, shaved, combed my hair with pomade and dressed for the day in white shirt with celluloid collar--as always, wrestling with the collar button at the back of my neck --a gray broadcloth suit with a vest, and a narrow, black silk tie as was the style of the day for a young working man.

  I was already seated at the dining room table, studying the notes made the evening before when Judith came downstairs to prepare breakfast. After we had eaten and Judith had seen to Mother's needs, we discussed the notes and the sagacity of our having taken dear Florence into our "team". We did acknowledge the fact the she had served some useful purpose by remembering that Grandfather had been "created".

  I had fished my watch from my vest pocket and consulted it several times that morning, fearing that Florence might not be on time. To my astonishment, Florence tapped the door knocker at precisely ten-thirty. She appeared bright-eyed that morning and greeted Judith and me with a broad smile. In fact, she looked especially fetching in her light blue gown and matching bonnet which was trimmed with tiny flowers and satin ribbons, setting off her blond curls and blue eyes. Her outfit was a striking contrast to sister Judith's modest dark blue dress and simple brimmed straw hat that was decorated with a single navy ribbon around the crown. Her dark brown hair was coiffed into a bun at her nape, making her appear more mature than her cousin.

  Judith made arrangements for a young lady who lived next door to stay overnight with mother. Then we ate an early lunch and Judith, with some help from Florence, packed a basket with sandwiches and a jar of tea for our evening meal should we need it.

The three of us walked to Mr. Herkheimer's office to find his door locked. We should have expected that, considering that Conrad's twenty-four hours had not quite expired. We waited in the hallway outside Mr. Herkheimer's office, the ladies sat on a mahogany bench while I paced back and forth, fedora in hand, waiting for news of Conrad's success or lack thereof.

Some fifteen minutes later the big door at the base of the stairs opened. Mr. Herkheimer entered and stomped up the stairs, a scowl on his face. Cousin Conrad followed, red of face and shouting loudly. "I almost had it! I know I did, and so do you. But you couldn't wait one more minute! Let me assure...," he caught sight of the ladies and me waiting beside the door, doffed his bowler in deference to the ladies then shook his cigar in our direction as he continued. "Let me assure you that I fully intend to contest the result of this little fiasco, no matter what the outcome!"

Mr. Herkheimer produced a large ring of keys from his pocket and started to unlock his office door, then turned and leveled a piercing gaze at cousin Conrad. "And let me assure you, Mr. Thompson, that it will do you no good whatsoever. Your grandfather's will has been reviewed and its provisions are incontestable. Good day, Mr. Thompson."

Cousin Conrad glared at the four of us. "We'll see," he grumbled, "We'll see." He jammed his bowler low over his eyes, clamped the stub of a cigar between his teeth, stomped down the stairs and out the door.

We went into Mr. Herkheimer's office where he apologized for his outburst and started to explain, then stopped himself. I had the feeling that Mr. Herkheimer's time with Cousin Conrad had been, to say the least, less than enjoyable. Mr. Herkheimer reviewed the rules with us, excusing himself for yawning while doing so. He had had no sleep in the past twenty-four hours and did not look forward to none for the next twenty-four.

Exactly on the hour Mr. Herkheimer rose and, speaking in a gentle voice, asked, "Ladies, Mr. Thompson, shall we be off?"

As we walked the short distance to the mansion, Florence lagged behind, humming a simple tune and looking at birds, trees, houses, clouds or anything else that attracted her attention, and twirling the parasol that rested on her shoulder.

We arrived at the mansion and Mr. Herkheimer unlocked the door with a key from the large ring. We stepped inside and saw that the furniture had been covered with cloths to protect it from the thin patina of dust that covered everything in the rooms.

We had decided earlier that we would make a quick search of the other rooms in the house and then direct our attention to the locked study that Sister Judith had remembered. I would look through the first floor rooms, Judith would inspect the second floor and Florence, the third. There were fewer rooms on that floor, thus, less to distract Florence from her mission.

Florence hesitated as we began our hunt. "Cousin John," she asked, "what are we searching for?"

I hurriedly explained that the object was a small urn... a sort of vase with a lid and about so high...I indicated the height with my hands... and filled with ashes.

Her face lit with a broad smile. "Oh...all right," she said, lifted her skirt slightly and tapped up the stairs.

An hour later we gathered at the base of the stairs and I asked Mr. Herkheimer to unlock the door to the mysterious room next to the dining room. We entered a dark, musty space. The four coal oil lamps in the room had been filled by Mr. Herkheimer in preparation for the searches. The dust in the room had been disturbed, and there was a strong odor of cigar smoke. Obviously, Cousin Conrad had been in the library.

The room was large, some thirty feet long, more than twenty feet in width, and windowless. A huge carved mahogany desk was near the fireplace at the end of the room and there were several large chairs around the desk...most likely the place where Grandfather had negotiated many deals.

Book shelves lined the walls floor to ceiling save the space taken by the door and the fireplace. There was not an empty space on them. The books were shelved in alphabetical order by author's name; Aeschylus' trilogies; Aristotle; six volumes by William Ellery Channing; "Pickwick Papers"; Hawthorne's "Twice Told Tales"; Plato, Shakespeare; Tennyson; "Walden" by Thoreau; Johann Wyss' "Swiss Family Robinson";"....and many, many others whose names I did not recognize.

I decided that my best strategy was to look through those books in which the author might treat on the subject of logic ...Aristotle, Plato ...who else? I would look for letters or notations, anything that would provide...what had he called it...the key to his riches?

Grandfather's letter had led us to believe that the key to his riches would be found somewhere among those books...somewhere between Abelard and Zola. I stood and looked in awe at the several hundreds of books on the shelves between the ones written by those two authors.

Tall glass cases stood back to back in a row down the center of the room. They were filled with hundreds of urns and tankards that Grandfather had collected during his many sojourns in countries around the world.

Judith began with the containers on the desk top and the contents of the drawers, even though we were sure that Conrad had done the same.

I began a search of the books...a near impossible task in the few hours allotted for our search. I tried to take a logical, organized approach to my work, bowing to Grandfather's references to logic in his letter.

Florence, and now Judith, looked in the collection of urns and tankards for Grandfather's ashes. They, or a clue to their location, had to be in that room...somewhere in that room.

After completing their search of the urns and tankards, Judith and Florence began to search through books on the lower shelves while I searched those on the higher shelves using the rolling ladder to reach the top several shelves.

Our search continued for hours. Occasionally, I would climb down from the rolling ladder to rest. My calves and my feet ached from my standing so long on the narrow rungs.

After asking permission of the young ladies, I had removed my suit jacket, and later, after again asking their permission, I had lowered my tie.

Our remaining hours were becoming fewer and fewer, but we continued our search. Too soon, by my watch, only thirty minutes remained. We were weary to the bone and our eyes ached from searching in the dim light of the coal oil lamps.

We could discern the sounds of heavy snoring coming from the next room where attorney Herkheimer sat in a dining room chair, his chin resting on the top of his bulging vest.

Florence, having grown weary from the long hours, had shown decreasing interest in our quest and was enchanted by paintings of birds in a large text by Mr. Audubon.

Weary and exasperated, Judith took her notes from the top of Grandfather's desk, plopped herself down on the floor in a most unladylike position and began, once more, to read the notes aloud, "Aristotle, premises, deductive logic, inductive logic. Between Abelard and Zola. Reverend Lumbard said it at my funeral..."

"Ashes to ashes...dust to dust, Reverend Lombard said that at Daddy's funeral," said Florence, who had abandoned the bird studies and was stabbing about in the fireplace with an iron poker she had taken from a rack on the hearth, probing the remnants of a fire that had last glowed twenty years before.

"What did you say?" I asked

"Ashes to ashes, dust to dust," Florence repeated

I pondered the words that Florence had repeated. I pulled out my watch and found that only ten minutes remained of our allotted twenty-four hours. I heard Mr. Herkheimer stirring about in the dining room. Judith and I looked at each other.

"Ashes to ashes", Judith repeated, "Could it be...?"
She looked at me and then we both looked at the fireplace where Florence was teasing the ashes.

I jumped from the third rung of the ladder and dashed to the fireplace with Judith close behind. "Zola," I shouted, pointing to the books on the left side of the fireplace. "Abelard." I pointed to the right side. "Between Abelard and Zola!"

"In the fireplace!" Judith shouted to Florence. "Help us look in here...in the fireplace!"

We felt for loose bricks...the face of the fireplace, the sides. I ran to the rolling ladder and pushed it to one side of the fireplace, climbed it and pushed and pulled at bricks to the ceiling and as far across the face as I could reach. I unhooked the ladder, carried it to the other side of the fireplace, and repeated my search. Nothing. The mantle. Anything that was loose. Anything that would move. Five more minutes, I estimated, no more!

I dropped to my knees and began feeling the fire bricks inside the fireplace and then up the chimney. My hands and the sleeves of my white shirt were black. Loose soot fell on my face and I shook it free, not wanting to deter my searching fingers even one second.

My body was half inside the fireplace and my arm was stretched up the chimney as far as I could reach. I felt a small ledge in the brick and my fingers closed around a smooth object. I could barely reach it with one hand. I carefully gripped it and lowered my hand. It was a small black urn. It had been virtually invisible against the black of the chimney soot.

I turned and sat on the hearth between Judith and cousin Florence who were both on their knees, their hands and faces smudged from their search of the fireplace. They were jabbering excitedly and laughing.

I carefully lifted the lid from the urn. Judith's and Florence's heads bumped mine as we all tried to see inside the urn at the same time.

Ashes, gray ashes, were inside, and in the center of those ashes, its end protruding, was just what Grandfather had told us we would find...a key with the words "City National Bank" engraved into its surface...the key to his riches.

I looked up and saw Mr. Herkheimer standing in the doorway, his watch in his hand and a broad smile on his face. "Well, Mr. Thompson...ladies, I do believe that you have found your late Grandfather's ashes...and a very valuable key as well." He looked about the room. "It seems that there should be no reason now for you to carefully replace everything in your Grandfather's..." he looked at the three of us..."your library. That can be taken care of later. For now, why don't you go and freshen up and meet me at the bank in an hour. I'm sure you are anxious to find out what you Grandfather left you. We can take care of that rather quickly and then I believe I shall go home, have a light luncheon and sleep for the next three days!" His belly bounced as he laughed at the thought.

Some of Grandfather's hints had been helpful and others appeared to have been made for the folly of confusing the searchers. His ashes were found between Abelard, the name of the first author in the collection and Zola, the last. Abelard was just to the right of the fireplace and Zola on the left. The fireplace, and Grandfather's, ashes were between Abelard and Zola.

We could have found the urn containing Grandfather's ashes sooner had we applied simple logic and looked where ashes are most often found...in a fireplace. Reverend Lombard had said it, "Ashes to ashes...dust to dust."

My sister Judith and I went to our home and cousin Florence departed in the general direction of her house.

Judith washed the soot stains from her hands and face, changed her dress and took care of mother's needs. I cleaned myself, changed my shirt and tie, and brushed the dust and the few soot marks from my trousers.

We left the house only ten minutes before it was time to meet Lawyer Herkheimer. We set a rapid pace to the bank and entered to find Cousin Florence seated on a bench just inside the door. She sat primly in the same light blue gown and bonnet, her face, hands and dress still smudged with soot.

"Oh, hello Judith. Hello, John," she said, her face lighting with a smile. "I decided that we might get into some more soot or dust or something as we tried to find out what the key would unlock, so I thought I would just wait until we're finished, then I'll go home and bathe." Her face flushed as she said the word "bathe" in my presence.

The key unlocked a large teakwood case locked in the vault. Inside were several hundred thousand dollars in bills along with stock certificates, bonds, deeds to the mansion and other properties, and a tome written by grandfather that treated on the proper management of these assets.

We had Mr. Herkheimer draw up documents dividing everything into four equal parts, less a sizable trust set up for the establishment and operation of the Jeremiah Thompson Home for Unwed Mothers and Orphaned children. We offered Cousin Conrad his share, but he snorted and grumbled something to the effect that he would take legal action. He has since left town and taken employment as a traveling salesman with a wholesale hardware company. His share waits in the vault.

Yes, my dear friend, that is how sister Judith and I, and more recently--since the death of her mother--cousin Florence, have come to live in this fine mansion. Come, let me show you Grandfather's library. As a bibliophile, I am sure you too will find much of value-between Abelard and Zola.

The Artwork

The kid kneels on the sidewalk and studies his artwork. The eyes. Not right. Too big.

He leans forward and scrubs the round, heavy chalk marks from the concrete with the sleeve of his jacket. Another hole in the jacket and another dirty spot. No matter. Just one more hole and some more dirt.

A dog barks down the alley beyond the junk car, the brown-stained mattress and the shards of broken wine bottles.

Two short, thin, straight lines for eyes that never looked at him, never saw the world as it was, never looked to a future, drawn with the stub of chalk filched from the classroom.

Below the short, straight lines: two round, heavy chalk marks, close together. Nostrils that flared with anger.

A block away, a police car, then an ambulance scream of someone's disaster.

The kid kneels on the sidewalk and studies his artwork.

The mouth. A big circle. A shouting, yelling, cursing circle that never talked gently or sang sweetly to him.

The hat drawn low -- close over the short, thin, straight lines that never looked at him.

Upstairs, a man and a woman scream obscenities at each other.

The kid kneels on the sidewalk and studies his artwork.

Chains. Gold chains. Lots of gold chains. No gold - no yellow - the pilfered stub of white will have to do. Loops. Like practicing e's in class. E's all strung together from one side of the neck to the other.

A straight line at each wrist. Cuffs of a long-sleeved shirt to cover the needle scars.

Shoes. The chalk held flat scrubs in white shoes. White running shoes. Shoes for running away.

"You draw that yourself?" a classmate asks from behind.

The kid nods. "Uh huh."

"That's pretty good, but he don't have no ears."

The kid kneels on the sidewalk and studies his artwork. "Don't need no ears if you don't never listen to nobody, don't never hear nothin' nobody says."

"Who is it?"

"My Daddy."

"You draw all that?"

"I drew the hard part. The police did the easy part. They drew that line around him while he was still layin' here."

"You draw good."

The kid kneels on the sidewalk and studies his artwork.

Dowd's War

TAT-TAT-TAT-TAT TAT-TAT-TAT
Private Dowd dropped to the ground.
Flattened his body.
TAT-TAT-TAT-TAT TAT-TAT-TAT-TAT
Where had it come from?
Somewhere behind.
He felt for his helmet.
TAT-TAT-TAT-TAT
His helmet was gone.
TAT-TAT-TAT-TAT
Where was it coming from?
Somewhere behind.
Behind to his right.
Four o'clock?
Five o'clock?
TAT-TAT-TAT TAT-TAT
The gritty soil dug into his cheek.
When was he going to hear that thunk?
That thunk of a mortar round dropped into the tube, followed by an ear-shattering, firey, ripping, tearing, killing explosion.
TAT-TAT-TAT-TAT-TAT
Alone. Where were his buddies?
Wilson? Tigue? Dunn? Zook? Alone?
Semper-Fi.
TAT-TAT-TAT-TAT
Grenade.
When was a grenade going to arc through the air, bounce on the hard ground and roll menacingly close before…
TAT-TAT-TAT-TAT
Where were his buddies?
Semper-Fi
Dowd raised his head slightly and looked around.

Lifted his head higher.
Where were they?
His buddies?
TAT-TAT-TAT-TAT
Semper-Fi Back there.
Some were still back there.
Would always be back there.
He sat up, wiped dirt and sweat from his face, looked around.
Flowers, trees, fresh mown grass, grandchildren's toys, wife's gardening tools.
When would Dowd's war end?
A woodpecker, flashing its blood-red head flitted to another tree.
TAT-TAT-TAT-TAT TAT-TAT-TAT

THE THEORY

The flight attendant closed and locked the door, then reopened it and let one man in. His attaché case was partly open and he juggled it along with his umbrella, his boarding pass, and a handful of papers.

The attendant motioned him to the seat next to mine. I had seen him sitting in the waiting area before we boarded. He had been sorting through a sheaf of papers and making marks here and there. His clothing was rumpled and he had paid no attention to the fact that his heavy wool trousers were wicking up water from the tip of the umbrella that was caught in their cuff. Our departure had been delayed because of bad weather, but he never seemed to take notice of the announcements that periodically grumbled through the p.a. system.

The 737 protested its trip down the runway; the ground disappeared into gray cloud before the wheels were retracted. The flight became rougher with every few feet the airplane climbed into the lightning punctuated sky. Rain slashed across the window. The plane bounced and the tail end tried to swap places with the front end amid loud bangs and rattles.

I looked at the man next to me. He had unfastened his seatbelt--if he had ever fastened it--and was again sifting through his papers.

Flying in stormy weather is one of my pet hates. I needed something to soothe my nerves. The attendants weren't serving anything, so scotch was out of the question. Conversation would have to do.

"Going to Orlando?" I asked, trying to appear composed.

He looked at me. He bounced a couple of inches off his seat and his case bounced several more inches off his lap as heavy turbulence hammered our aluminum cocoon.

"Orlando? Oh yes, Orlando." He made a turning motion with a finger as though trying to reel out the words. "I have an important meeting in Orlando tomorrow morning at nine, or ten. Doctor Faulkner is going to send someone to meet me. He will know what time I have to meet with the others at the University.

"I am Doctor Julius Detwiler. I have a meeting tomorrow morning with Doctor Faulkner, Dean of the Department of Science. Later, I will address a group of scientists on my theory of finite oscillation velocity molecular fission. Mostly skeptics, I'm afraid. Are you familiar with my theory of finite oscillation velocity molecular fission?"

The plane dropped for what seemed to be a thousand feet to the accompaniment of bangs, rattles and screams. Some of the overhead compartments popped open and blankets, pillows, bags, sacks and a couple of toys cascaded to the floor. Dr. Detwiler stayed up as the plane went down. He landed on the arm of his seat. With no apparent discomfort, he shifted back into his place.

"No," I said, "I'm not familiar with your theory of finite whatever, but don't you think you should fasten your seatbelt?"

"It is very simple," he said, ignoring my question. "In fact, the title is so descriptive that it is self explanatory," he said as the plane lurched again. The motion lifted him half into my seat and caused his thick, gold-rimmed glasses to fall into my lap.

"Your seatbelt," I began, "Don't you think you should..."

"Really quite simple." he said as he recovered his glasses and hooked them over his ears. More turbulence caused papers to fly out of his case and his umbrella to sail upward. He grabbed the umbrella, stuffed it between his body and the armrest, and casually retrieved some of his papers. "Have you ever dropped a coin, heard it hit the floor at your feet, but could never find it?"

"Well, yes", I began, "but don't you think you should..."

"Ha! Then you have experienced it!" he exclaimed delightfuly. "You have experienced finite oscillation velocity molecular fission. You and thousands--no, millions of others have experienced finite oscillation velocity molecular fission without knowing what it was."

I looked at his flopping seatbelt and fought the urge to reach over and strap him down before he crashed against the ceiling.

"You see," he continued, "my theory states that every object has a finite oscillation velocity. If an object is thrown or dropped with an oscillating motion--a violent twisting, tumbling motion--the molecules that make up that object can be disturbed to the extent that fission--that is, separation--of those molecules may occur. When this takes place, the molecules dissipate and the object no longer exists. It literally disappears."

I tried to smile in spite of the continuous lurching of the airplane...and my stomach. "Is that why one sock disappears in the washing machine?"

Doctor Detwiler looked at me as though he either hadn't heard what I had asked, or had never had one sock disappear in the washing machine.

"In some cases the dissipation is incomplete. In seconds the oscillation slows and the molecules assume their original positions. Which explains why you may not be able to find an object immediately after you drop it, but it will be right in front of you moments later."

I couldn't believe what I was hearing. What little I retained from a high school physics class told me that Detwiler's theory was difficult to accept. Neither could I believe that this little man was discussing his theory so impassively during a flight that would make an aerobatics champion up-chuck in his cockpit.

"You see," he continued as lightning flashbulbed the sky, "molecular fission can happen to any object, even to animate objects. You can understand how my theory explains the unsolved disappearances of many humans. The person who was walking across a field in clear view one second and was gone the next merely fell or jumped with a particular twisting motion--oscillation--that caused the dissipation of the molecules that made up that person's body. Alien spacecraft are not involved--as those less informed might suppose."

The airplane shook violently, accompanied by an assortment of cracks, clangs, vibrations and screams.

"Do you mean that people disappear in the same way that a cuff link or a coin disappears?" I asked, trying to ignore my queasy stomach.

"Yes, of course. Humans and animals are made up of molecules the same as cuff links or coins. The molecules can separate just the same as ...."

Abruptly, the right wingtip was pointing toward the ground. The tail swapped angles with the nose and the plane was heading for the ground. One equilibrium-shattering move and the left wing pointed toward somebody's farm a few thousand feet below.

Something wet spattered my face.

The engines screamed, the wind screamed and every female and some of the men screamed. Books, bags, blankets, air sickness bags, and a toupee flew about as though caught in a whirlwind. Oxygen masks popped from their doors and whirled like yellow fetuses twirled on plastic umbilicals.

The airplane began a tight, fast spin to the left. Centrifugal force pulled me away from the window. The noise was like dozens of heavy-metal rock bands playing at the same time with all their amplifiers turned up to peak cacophony. After too many turns to count, the spinning slowed, and then stopped. The nose started to come up, as did my lunch. My head ached; my ears felt like they were ready for total blowout. I swallowed hard and looked out the window. The sight of cars on a divided highway a few hundred feet below told me that if the plane had made two or three more turns, those cars would have been driving around big chunks of aluminum.

Seconds later we popped out of the clouds into bright sunlight and unbelievably smooth air. With a click and a hiss of static the pilot's voice came over the intercom in the normal bored-airline-pilot monotone, something about a little rough air...passengers remain seated...would be landing in fifteen minutes... any injured passengers would deplane first...keep seatbelts fastened. I was hearing but not really listening.

The pilot's words reminded me that Doctor Detwiler's seatbelt had not been fastened. I turned to see if he was all right. His umbrella was open in his seat. Its sudden opening had spattered me with rainwater.

Doctor Detwiler wasn't there. I snapped open my seat belt, stood up and looked in the seats in front of me and behind me. I looked across the aisle, up and down the aisle. A flight attendant appeared, her uniform rumpled and her silver wings askew.

"Doctor Detwiler is missing," I shouted, "He was here a minute ago; now he's gone!"

"Please sit down and fasten your seatbelt," she said with typical flight attendant authority. "Maybe he went to the restroom. This flight has been enough to make anybody ...anybody have to go to the restroom." She pushed back the curtain separating the passenger sections and went forward to minister to the high-paying passengers.

I picked up a sheet of paper from the doctor's seat and read: Julius Detwiler Ph.D. THEORY OF FINITE OSCILLATION VELOCITY MOLECULAR FISSION. I didn't check the restrooms.

I was the last passenger off the airplane. The waiting area was crowded. Passengers hugged people who had come to meet them. Some were crying; others seemed to be in a daze. A young man in tee shirt, jeans and Reeboks held up a piece of cardboard with felt tip-scribbled letters: DR. J. DETWILER.

I stopped in front of him. "Doctor Detwiler won't be coming," I said.

I started to walk away, then turned back and said, "Just tell them that his theory is right."

Tunnels

"Look Jenny, look at the mountains." Glenda said to our daughter riding in the back seat.

Jenny stretched as high as she could against her seatbelt and looked out the window. "Uh huh," she said, not showing a great deal of excitement over the beautiful vista of Smoky mountains framed by the car window. A six-year-old can become bored after a short time and we were on our way home after two weeks of looking at mountains around our rented cabin. We were taking a scenic road from the cabin into north Georgia.

Jenny settled back in the seat and began bouncing worn, stuffed Peter Rabbit on her knee.

After five minutes or so I heard Jenny squirming in her seat. She stretched against her seatbelt again and looked out the window. "Mamma," she said, "did God make all those mountains?"

"Yes, Honey, God made all of them and lots more."

"And God made birds and squirrels and sunshine, and clouds and everything else, didn't he, Mamma?"

"Yes, Honey, he made everything."

Jenny held Peter Rabbit facing her and spoke to him in a most authoritative voice, "Peter, God made you and me and everything else. Even those mountains."

I maneuvered around another of many tight curves and aimed the car toward the entrance to a tunnel.

"Daddy! Daddy! It's dark! What happened to the sun?"

I laughed. "Nothing, Jenny, We're just going through a tunnel."

"A tunnel? What's a tunnel?"

"A tunnel is a hole through a mountain. When they are building a road and a mountain is in the way, they just cut a hole through it so cars can go through instead of a long way around."

Jenny sat back, deep in thought about my answer. A few minutes later we went through another tunnel. Jenny ducked her head, moaned "Ooooh," and squeezed Peter Rabbit close. Before we got to the Georgia state line we went through three more tunnels, and each time Jenny would, "Oooooh," close her eyes, duck her head and hug Peter Rabbit.

"Daddy, are we going through any more tunnels?"

"I don't think so. Pretty soon we'll be getting on a big, wide highway and there won't be any tunnels on it"

"Mamma, did God make tunnels?"

"No, God doesn't make tunnels, People make tunnels."

"How do they make tunnels?"

Glenda turned in her seat to face Jenny. "Oh, they take big drills and cut into the mountain like Daddy drilled holes in boards when he was making that swing for you under the big tree in the backyard. And then they use dynamite to blow out big pieces of rock. They dig out all the rock and dirt and then they put the road right through the mountain."

"Ooooh, I don't like tunnels!"

"Why not, Honey?"

"Because they are dark, and I think they hurt."

"They hurt?"

"Uh huh. When they cut holes in the mountain I think it hurts…like this."

Jenny leaned forward as far as she could and put her little hand on the top of the seat back. I glanced at the hand and saw a finger with cartoon figures circling a plastic bandage. I chuckled, "Maybe it does, Jenny, you may be right."

We hit the Interstate in north Georgia, stopped for lunch and some shopping in Atlanta. Later, a stop for gasoline and restrooms. Dinner and sleep was at a motel in South Georgia. A quick breakfast and we were back on the fast, crowded Interstate. By noon we were a hundred miles from home. Both Glenda and Jenny were dozing, tired from the trip and the Interstate monotony.

Glenda roused, rubbed her eyes and yawned. I'm sorry, I should stay awake to keep you company, but I'm having a hard time keeping my eyes open." We passed a large green and white sign showing the name of the next town. "This is where you grew up, isn't it?"

"Just outside town. Our farm was a couple miles outside town." Memories flickered through my mind as I drove. "You know what I'd like to do? I'd like to cut across to I-95, go out the road that we took to the farm and then through the National forest to the coast."

"Fine with me," Glenda responded "I'd like to see something new instead of six lanes of speeding cars."

I turned onto a narrow blacktop and soon saw familiar landmarks. Huge, ancient oaks lined the road.

"Daddy! Daddy! Stop! I want to go through that tunnel again!"

I glanced in the rear view mirror. "We didn't go through a tunnel, Jenny. There aren't any tunnels here."

"Yes we did, Daddy. Please...I want to go through that tunnel again."

I looked at Glenda who had turned to look behind us for the tunnel Jenny was talking about. She looked at me with an expression and a shrug that said, *I don't know either.* "It's still early," she said, "Let's go back and see what she's talking about."

There was no traffic, so I turned the car around in the road. I drove back slowly, waiting for Jenny to let me know when we got to her "tunnel." Again she was stretching to see out the window.

Here, Daddy! Here. Stop Daddy! I want to get out and see the tunnel." I stopped the car on the side of the road and we all got out.

Jenny stood in the middle of the road and looked all around at the giant old oaks. The oaks stood close together with roots dug deep giving strength and security. They were like great ladies in billowy gowns holding hands across the way, high above the road.

"See, Daddy, it's a tunnel!"

It was a tunnel...a cool dark tunnel of trees. I looked about and recognized it as the place I would stop to rest after pumping my bike up the steep hill past the cemetery. I had never thought of it as a tunnel those years back, just a cool place for a short rest.

Jenny stretched her arms as far as she could reach and turned around and around, looking first at the tall trees and then at the plants at the sides of the road and then at the ground. Her blond hair shined against the dark and her eyes sparkled with wonder.

"I like this tunnel." Jenny announced. "I see trees and all kinds of green leaves and I can see birds, and there are squirrels. There's a spider up there and I can see some bees. I can see little pieces of the sky and pieces of clouds and there are little spots of sunshine. I see little bugs on the bushes and ants on the ground. I like this tunnel.

"God made this tunnel!"

MORNING MIST

A splash of white
In the early gray.
Silent, measured steps
as it searches, seeks.
A downward thrust
of a golden spear.
To rise with writhing silver
impaled.
A whisper of sound far away.
Snowy wings spread, lift the egret
Quietly
into
the

The Readin'

1935

'Bout this time last year my wife, Lurlene, dragged me down to the town library to one of them "Readin's." I thought it might be pretty good, figurin' that they'd read somethin' like an article from Popular Mechanics on how to fix a twenty-year-old John Deere tractor, but I found out that what it is, is that some fat lady you don't know gets up and reads out loud somethin' you don't understand that was written by somebody you never heard of.

Well, last week Lurlene told me that they was havin' another readin' at the library and she wanted me to go with her, and I said no and then hell no and then I said OK because I could see she was goin' to throw one of her fits and I didn't feel like goin' through one of her long, quiet, dry weeks.

The library is just two rooms in Miz. Sistrunk's house that used to be ole Doc Sistrunk's office before he died back five, six years ago. He had some shelves in there and quite a few books, so Miz. Sistrunk had ole Dooley Cass come in an' build some more shelves and called it a town library. It ain't bad for a town this size, must have two, three, hundred books about all kinds of things.

When we got there, they had put some foldin' chairs and some of Miz Sistrunk's dining room chairs in the back room that usually don't have anything in it, and up front they had one of them tall, skinny tables like the Reverend Hawkins stands behind when he preaches on Sunday mornin'. I told Lurlene that I wanted to sit in the back row near the door so there wouldn't be nobody behind us to see if I kinda dozed off and Lurlene had to poke me in the ribs with her elbow like last time. She said no, she wanted a good seat up front and I said that if I had to come, I was goin' to sit where I damnwell wanted to, and besides, there weren't but three rows of chairs, so we sat in the back row near the door.

The readin' started about like the last one-some little old lady named Talley, from Live Oak, wearin' a flowered dress and a little hat with a veil on top, who was what they called the "visitin' writer" because she had got an article printed in the Live Oak Weekly Ledger about growin' geraniums, read somethin' I didn't understand that was written by somebody I never heard of.

The next one to read was Mr. Wooley that teaches literature at the high school, the one with thick glasses and curly hair and weak wrists and talks kinda like a girl and looks like he'd say "Oh my goodness" when most men would say sonofabitch, and wears them crinkly Montgomery Ward seersucker suits and bow ties when nobody else in town wears bow ties 'cept that fat, white-haired lawyer, Harley Whitley, that defends colored folks in front of a judge all week and then calls them niggers and puts on a hood and a robe so nobody will know who he is- 'cept everybody does- and burns crosses on weekends.

That teacher got up and he read a poem about a blacksmith that had arms as strong as iron bands. While I listened pretty good, it didn't mean much to me 'cause the only blacksmith I ever knew was old Pop Grimley, and he was a little, wiry kind of fellow with bad teeth and a lot of hair in his ears.

Miz Sistrunk got up next and she read a story by some woman who said she'd like to have a wife to do all those things that wives are 'sposed to do, and the more I listened the more I figured out that she wasn't really writin' about women but she was sort of writing out of the corner of her mouth about what she thought men should do and the way she thought they ought to be.

Yesterday morning I was out in the privy doing my everymorning and I got to thinking about that woman wantin' a wife. I do a lot of thinking when I'm in the privy doin' my everymorning 'cause it's quiet out there and it's cool 'cause it's back up under a big oak tree, and Lurlene never comes out there to bother me.

What I got to thinkin' was that if that woman wanted to have her a wife to do things she didn't want to do then I oughta be able to have a husband to do the things I don't want to do.

First, I'd let him work them night and weekend overtime hours down at the feed store when we have truckloads of feed an' fertilizer come in that have to be unloaded and he'd be the one that would snuff that feed dust up his nose 'til he couldn't hardly breathe and have that dust run under his collar and down his back and mix with sweat so it feels like biscuit dough mixed with them little pointy things off of prickly pears. When Mr. Squires, the owner of the feed store, said, "Boys y'all gotta work tonight and unload that truck load of feed an' fertilizer," I'd just tell him to wait a minute, I gotta call my husband 'cause he's the one that works them overtime hours. And that husband of mine, he'd do it without grumblin' 'cause we need that extra money to buy new shoes and school clothes for the younguns, and a washin' machine so Lurlene won't have to bend over a wash tub and a scrub board no more.

I think I'd let him be the one to castrate them little boar pigs. I don't like to do that. I got hit with a ball one time when me and Corbett Rudd and Frank Mulkey were playing with an old stringy softball with the cover wore off and a table leg for a bat and Corbett threw that ball hard and low and ...well, I just think it hurts them little pigs more than some folks figure and I just plain don't like to do it.

He'd go with us to them family reunions up at Lurlene's aunt Loodie's place outside Micanopy. Now I'd eat my share 'cause they always have lots of mighty good eatin' 'cept for that casserole thing that Lurlene's cousin Myrtle always makes with all kind of things mixed up in it like asparagus and mushrooms and green beans cut the wrong way, and Lurlene's sister Pauline's potato salad that she always puts olives in. But I'd take that husband along so he could sit in the parlor with all them kin and listen to them tell about all the things they did when they was kids that I've done heard a couple hundred times or so, and I'd go 'cross the road to the pond behind the Freewill Baptist Church and catch a few bream or skip some rocks across it, or maybe go and read the names and dates on some tomb stones in that little cemetery behind the church.

But that husband would come in mighty handy when we started home from that reunion. I'd let him drive all the way and I'd sit over on the right hand side and I'd lean my head up against the window and sleep all the way, like Lurlene usually does, and when we got home way after dark, 'cause we left three hours later than Lurlene said we would, he'd be the one that'd say, "Naw," when Lurlene said, "Now, that weren't so bad, were it?" And then he could go feed the chickens and the hogs and the cows and gather eggs and do the milkin' while Lurlene and me put away all the eats we brought back from her aunt Loodie's and gave the younguns their baths and got them to bed.

That husband would do all the painting around the place. There's always wasp nests up under the eaves that you gotta burn out and I always get stung a couple times 'cause some of them wasps get real riled up when you try to do that. He'd be the one that would get the crick in his neck from lookin' up to paint under them eaves, and the one that would feel like he got a bad sunburn when he had to scrub all the paint drippins' off his hands and arms and face and neck with turpentine.

Lordeee, would I ever let him kill chickens for Sunday dinner. Them little biddies hatch out and they're all soft and yellow and you go out twice a day and feed them and they go cheep cheep all around you and you can reach down and rub their backs and then, when they're all growed up, you're supposed to go out there and pick one of them up by the legs and stretch her neck out on that old stump by the barn and take your axe and... well, I sure wouldn't do that no more.

Muckin' out the the barn and the chicken coop. That's another thing he could do. Now I like cows and I like chickens, but I sure don't like the way they mess up their stalls and their coops. After a while, that smell just begins to wear on you.

He'd be the one that Lurlene would run to with her face all red when I come home from work, and she'd yell at him to go in there and give them boys a good whippin' 'cause you can't believe what they done today, and he'd be the one to go an' do it, if it truly had to be done.

I sure hope he'd be able to fix things. Seems like a husband has to be able to fix anything even if he don't have the tools or the parts and don't have the slightest notion on how to fix it. I'd be happy to let him sweat and cuss over that twenty-year-old John Deere tractor under the shed, and he could try to keep our old Studebaker running.

He could chop wood for the fireplace and the old wood stove and he could get up before sunrise and build a fire in the fireplace while he froze his feet on that floor and his bottom felt cold as Billy-be-damned 'cause the button was missin' from the back of his long underwear.

He could mow the grass with that old, rusty, push mower and he could help Lurlene cook and set the table and wash the dishes and scrub the clothes and hang them out on the line in cold weather and sweep the floor, and do all them other things Lurlene says I ought to help her do. And he'd go to them church socials on Saturday night when I'm tired out from workin' all day.

Now there's some things he wouldn't do. I'd still do the sleepin' with Lurlene, and when she got to thinkin' about her Mama and how she missed her and started bawlin', I'd still be the one that would hold her and try to make her feel better.

I'd be the one to go the school and be proud when one of our kids was in a play or a ball game or graduated, and I'd be the one to sign their report cards when they got good grades. I'd be the one that would teach them how to do things like fishing and working with tools and playin' ball and how to respect women and the flag.

Lurlene and me would teach them to appreciate things that are just naturally around, like woods and rivers and lakes and wildflowers and blackberries and sunshine and rain and sunrise and sunset, and how to thank the Good Lord for all of them.

It would be up to me to tell them to stay in school and graduate instead of droppin' out like I did, and I'd be the one that would do my best to find a way for them to go to college if they want to.

Plowin'...now I'd keep on doin' the plowin'. Ain't nothing like walking a furrow behind a good mule on a purty morning, and smelling that dirt as it turns over. And if that's a real good mule, you have a lot of time for serious thinkin', 'cause that mule just naturally knows when to turn around, and where to set the next furrow and how to pull that plow along just right, not too fast, not too slow, just good and steady.

Tomorrow or the next day, or maybe next week, I'd take my daddy's rifle and Booger, my old blue-tick hound, out in the woods for the last time and do what I gotta do 'cause he's all eat up inside with the cancer, and near 'bout blind. That husband couldn't do that ...nobody but me could do that. And when I was diggin' a hole to put ole Booger in, I wouldn't care if that husband did think I was blubbering over a worthless ole fleabag when I really had tears in my eyes from some sand I'd kicked up with the shovel.

There's lots of things I'd let him do and there's lots of things I'd keep doin' if I had me a husband, but there's one thing for sure. From now on, he'd be the one to go with Lurlene to them "Readin's".

Poems

Non-Rhyming Couplet

The hunting eagle looks down and envies
The people their full bellies.
The people look up and envy
The eagle its freedom.

Two Couplets

The sky celebrates day's end brightly
With banners of gold and red.
While night steps in lightly
And the tired sun trudges off to bed.

Limerick

There once was a man who walked funny
His pockets were so filled with money.
But in spite of his walk
And garbled way he would talk
He never ever lacked for a honey.

Halloween 1938

When we lived on the farm we didn't go trick or treating. Not because we didn't want to but because the houses were so far apart that we would have spent more time walking in the dark than we would have spent trick and treating, and the only treats that some of the folks down the road could have offered would have been a slab of cold corn bread cooked with lard or a glass of warm buttermilk. I didn't like the taste of things cooked in lard, hated the taste of buttermilk and didn't even like the way a glass looked after anybody drank a glass of buttermilk.

It was kind of a surprise when the older boys who lived close enough around to get together at our house to try to think of something exciting to do on that chilly Halloween night in the late thirties. They sat under the big hickory trees that bordered the two-rut road that ran in front of our house, far enough away from the house so that Mom or Grandma couldn't hear their plotting and far enough away from me and Corbett Rudd, who had walked the mile from his house to get some fudge that Mom had promised, that we couldn't hear what they were planning and go tell Mom or Grandma.

Corbett and I knew the older boys were going to do something special so we sneaked out the back door, went north, then east through a small grove of pine saplings and crossed the road under the dark of a big oak that grew on the north border of our place, climbed the Baird's barbed wire fence and then headed back south, crawling under the cover of dog fennel that grew four or so feet high along the edge of the road.

When we stopped we could see my brother Charlie, Ray, Buford, and fat, curly-haired, pigeon-toed "Two Gun" whose real name was Eugene, but the older boys called him

"Two Gun" because when they were all younger and played cowboys and Indians he always had two cap pistols buckled around his chubby waist instead of one like everybody else.

We kept shushing each other and listening and finally, we heard the older boys talking about old man Junkins, who lived down the road, and his outhouse--or privy--or something else I'd best not repeat, and we stayed hidden in the bushes until our old dog, Flash, came snuffing across the road, wagging his tail, and stuck his wet nose in Corbett's ear and we got chased back to the house by the older boys.

Corbett and I decided we would rather stay at the house and eat fudge than follow the older boys and get into trouble when they caught us, which they would surely do, so we sat on the front steps and ate our fudge in the dark so the night bugs wouldn't be attracted to the porch light and land on our fudge, and we waited for my brother Charlie and Ray and Buford and "Two Gun" to come back and tell us about the fun they had tipping over old man Junkins' outhouse - or privy - or whatever.

Our fudge was finished and we were still licking our fingers when we heard a commotion down the road in the direction of old man Junkins' house. It didn't take long for us to realize that the noise was made by a lot of feet running hard and fast. We could tell that the runners were getting closer and then we could make out Buford, the lankiest of the bunch, cutting off the two-rut road and into the front yard, followed by my brother Charlie, then Ray and, after a little while, "Two Gun" who was huffing and stumbling in his pigeon-toed run and trying to yell for the others to wait. They each fell down on the floor as they reached the porch, gasping for breath and trying to talk, except "Two Gun" who fell down about ten feet before he got to the porch and skinned his knees on the rough coquina walk that led from the dirt driveway to the front steps.

They were all trying to talk at once at first and all Corbett and I could understand was something about screaming and screeching. After about five minutes, they got their breaths and they started to tell us--interrupting each other to amplify their terror--about how they had gone into the woods before they got to old man Junkins' house so they could creep along the bushes beside his old fence and into the shadows of the oak trees behind his house where the target was located. They swore that nobody knew they were there and that they hadn't made a sound except for "Two Gun" who had sneezed twice because he was allergic to dry grass in the fall.

Just as they got to the outhouse--or privy--or whatever, and started to whisper about which way it should be tipped, a horrible, blood-curdling, screaming, screeching, yowling sound came from inside the small building.

Buford said he ain't never heard no sound like that afore in his life and Ray said it was ten times worse than any screech owl he had ever heard and "Two Gun" said he wanted to go home and would anybody walk with him?

Since they had run away from the horrible, blood-curdling, screaming, screeching, yowling sound, the four swore Corbett and me to absolute secrecy under the threat that violation would be punishable by our being dunked head-first into the skunk-and-possum-hole, which was actually an old watering trough back in the woods where a house had been and into which a skunk and a possum had, in turn, fallen and drowned, forming a rather unpleasant appearing malodorous content after a couple of weeks.

A few days later, on the way home on the school bus, Corbett asked me if I could go down the road to his house to see the new pigs their old sow had had the day before, so I asked Mom and she said I could if I promised to be back home before five thirty and I changed from my school clothes to my play clothes, which were old school clothes, and Corbett and I headed down the road toward his house.

The Rudds lived about half a mile down the road on the other side of old man Junkins' place and as we got near old man Junkins' we started talking low and walking on the other side of the road.

Just as we got even with the house we heard it...the horrible, blood-curdling, screaming, screeching, yowling sound...and it was coming from the privy, or outhouse ...or whatever.

We ran, all stooped down like, into the dog fennels along the side of the road. The horrible, blood-curdling screaming, screeching, yowling sound continued-scratching, squealing, raspy, shrill...the sort of sound that crawls up your back and scuffs up the hair on the back of your neck.

We whispered back and forth about what we should do and finally decided that considering that it was daylight and nothing like that hurts you in the daylight; we should sneak around the fence line, like the older boys had done, and see if we could find out what was making that horrifying noise.

I figured that I had to be as brave as Corbett and he figured the same about me, so we crawled through blackberry bushes and wire grass and elderberry bushes -getting scratches and chiggers all over us- until we got within about eight feet from the door, which was about one-third open, and the screeching was louder and more hideous than ever.

Corbett whispered that we ought to move a little closer so we could see in the opening in the doorway when the terrible sounds stopped.

A long, thin stick slid out and slowly pushed the door full open as the hinges protested the movement with a raspy, rusty creak.

When we saw what was inside we started to run, but the sound of a loud voice stopped us in our tracks. "Hey boys, y'all like that?"

Old man Junkins was sitting on the two-holer, his old, stained felt hat pulled low over his eyes, his long underwear gaping at the back pulled up at the sides around his bottom, bib overhauls down around his worn brogans, half a Mason jar of home made whiskey between his feet, a fiddle in his left hand and the bow, which he had used to push the door open, in his right.

"Always wanted me a fiddle," he shouted in his, hoarse, whiskey-soaked voice, "My red-headed wife an' me, we went to town last saddy an' she went down to the feed store to get some chicken feed in some purple-flowered sacks she wanted for a Sunday-go-to-meetin' dress an' she took so long I went and got a pint in a sack and sat on a bench on the Courthouse square and ate boiled peanuts and drank whiskey till I got kinda drunk an' I started to walk down to the feed store to get her an' I saw this fiddle in a store winder an' I went in an' bought it. Three dollar. Old lady won't let me bring it in the house...says I kin bring it when I learn how to play "Listen to the Mockingbird" on it...makes me keep it out here...but I come out here an' play it when I want to. Y'all want to hear some more?"

Corbett and I looked at each other and started to laugh and old man Junkins started sawing on the fiddle again, making that horrible, blood-curdling, screaming, screeching, yowling sound before we could say anything.

I followed Corbett over the old fence and we started running toward the two-rut road, laughing so hard we couldn't run fast. We kept running and laughing until we got the other side of old man Junkins' property and then we fell down in the sandy dirt road and rolled around and laughed until our sides ached.

We never told my brother Charlie, or Ray or Buford or "Two Gun" about our experience at old man Jenkins' outhouse --or privy--or whatever, but now and then we would beg them, with pleading eyes, to tell us about what happened on that chilly Halloween night, and they would recite their tale, which got scarier and more horrible with each telling, and Corbett and I would listen like we were awe struck. And when they were finished we would go around to the other side of the house where they couldn't see or hear us and we would fall down in the sandy dirt and roll around and laugh until our sides ached.

THE BEST LAID PLAN

George Franklin had paused to unfold his handkerchief and place it over his wife's face before shoveling dirt into the hole. Again, he hesitated, and then stepped onto the loose soil to pack it firm. He shoveled more dirt from the pile on the sheet of black plastic where he had placed it when he dug the grave, and once again packed it with his rubber boot-covered feet. He continued until the dirt reached the level of the ground, then smoothed it with the back of the folding army shovel.

He lifted the sheet of plastic by the corners and carried it to the river bank, waded in and dumped the remaining dirt into the water. He rinsed the plastic, shook off the water, folded it, took it to his car and placed it in the trunk. He sat in the car and rested for a few minutes, puffing and wiping sweat from his brow with the clean, back side of his gloved hand.

The sliver of moon provided only faint light, and the dense foliage of the trees allowed little of that to filter through. He had to use his small flashlight to find the second piece of black plastic, from which he scooped up leaves and scattered them back over the grave site.

George stepped back to make sure that his work blended in with the natural cover of leaves. In the darkness he could not locate the grave. He turned on the flashlight and surveyed the area again, stooped and rearranged a few leaves.

At the rear of the car he used the flashlight to inventory the items he had used to bury Margaret. Beside each entry on the computer printout there was a single check mark. A second check was made as each item was accounted for: sheet, black plastic, 6'x6' for leaves; sheet, black plastic, 6'x6' for dirt from hole; rubber boots; folding shovel; cotton gloves.

George slipped on his shoes, closed the trunk lid and walked to the open door of the five-year-old Plymouth. He sat on the end of the seat, his feet on the ground, and rested for a few minutes to catch his breath, settle his nerves and regain his strength. Sweat ran down the side of his face. It had been the most strenuous work he had done for years--digging with the short-handled shovel, and shoveling the dirt to fill the hole, as quickly and quietly as possible. And it hadn't been easy for a sixty-six-year-old, over-weight man to carry the body of his wife who weighed twice what she had weighed when he had carried her over the threshold thirty-seven years before.

Thirty-seven long years. At first he had put up with her ways, assuring himself that she would learn to be more organized, to finish jobs, to put things away, to make lists, to follow those lists, to plan everything in detail, and to follow those plans precisely. But there had never been such a change in Margaret.

It had been his job as an Industrial Engineer to show others how to organize, how to plan, how to work in the most efficient manner. Work distribution, critical path analysis, PERT, time and motion studies, process charts, detailed record keeping, his work had become his way of life. Everything was studied, planned, carried out, recorded, and filed. George could quickly find a record of the cost of groceries, the price of an oil change, electric bills, water bills, amount put out for each item of expense -in detail- and end-of-month of cash-on-hand (wallet, purse and pocketbook) for the month of October, 1973, or for any other month or week for the past forty years.

The development of the personal computer had inspired George to even more detailed planning and record keeping.

He had anxiously waited until he was satisfied that there were enough computers on the market for him to make a detailed comparison of functions, program availability, repair records, and an array of other factors that he had plotted for many months on a grid carefully laid out on a giant sheet of paper meticulously attached with eight thumb tacks (from box three of drawer two) to the neat bulletin board hung with four screws and anchors (selected for their, tensile strength and load capability-times two) to the wall of the room he had designated his work room in their home, the locked room Margaret never visited except for an occasional run of the vacuum cleaner in a carefully orchestrated manner under George's watchful supervision.

Auto maintenance was performed on a monthly basis, with George fidgeting when an oil change, lubrication, check of brakes, belts, hoses, battery had to be delayed one day because the only mechanic George trusted didn't work on Sundays. Cars were traded when the odometers showed eighty-three thousand miles for a similar four door, six cylinder, straight shift, solid color, basic model. Only the one he sat in and the one he traded on it had air conditioning, and then only after denying that his increasing weight was the cause of his warm weather discomfort and "proving" that the average mean summer temperature in Atlanta had climbed two degrees over the preceding five years.

"Plan," he had told Margaret time after time. "Analyze. Organize your life. Planning is the secret to success. Write down your plan in detail and do not waver from that plan."

In spite of his constant counseling, Margaret was never inclined to take his advice. Not until a year ago. Margaret had mentioned that a neighbor had bought a new dishwasher, and hinted that she would like one. George had locked himself away in the evenings for a week and had emerged from his sanctuary to tell Margaret that by using store-brand dish detergent, turning the hot water heater down three degrees, and using Gilbreth motion economy principles in washing the dishes, they could save the money for a dishwasher in three years and seven months - money that would be invested at a high interest rate.

Soon afterward, when she had come home a half-hour late from grocery shopping, George had again provided guidance on planning properly, writing her plan and following that plan to assure that she would complete all required tasks, finish, and be home at a pre-determined time.

Margaret's eyes narrowed and her lips tightened. "George, I have done just that. I have planned something and written out my plan. Now leave me alone."

A look of surprise and a trace of a smile showed on George's stern face. "I would like to see your written plan, Margaret, to see if you have prepared it properly- in sufficient detail- and to see if it is a viable plan."

"George, it's my plan. I am satisfied that is viable and prepared in sufficient detail. I don't see your plans; you don't see mine," she said, and went to the kitchen.

He couldn't take her lack of organization, lack of planning and record keeping any more. And now, it was her attitude toward him. She had flared at him several times. She had called him cold and obsessive, and told him that she couldn't stand his nit-picking everything she did, said there had to be some changes or she would leave. George couldn't stand her lack of organization, lack of caring about cost, and her wastefulness. And he couldn't stand the thought of her leaving him- not because he would miss her especially, but because he knew that if she left, there would be months of calculating an equitable division of assets, and he knew, without a doubt, that her half would be squandered away because of her lack of organization, planning, and record keeping.

George knew that there had to be a way. His forced retirement at age sixty-five supplied the answer. Their house in Atlanta had appreciated to the point that--according to George's calculations-- the best move would be for them to sell it, retire to Florida where nobody knew them, buy a modest home in a small town, and invest the rest of the money. They had no children, no close relatives, and no real friends. If Margaret didn't show up at their new home, nobody would know that there had been a Mrs. Franklin.

It was possible, George thought, only through detailed planning and scrupulous adherence to that plan.

For several weeks, George would lock himself in his work room in the evening, call his plan up on the screen of his computer, study it in detail, and add, change, or delete entries as he fine-tuned it. Perfect. It had to be perfect, detailed, and one-hundred-percent viable.

The house sold forty-two days after George put the "For sale by owner" sign in the front yard- to avoid a real estate agent's fee; and George had driven alone to Florida and bought a modest home near enough to the coast to derive the cooling benefit of an ocean breeze, but far enough inland to avoid the high price and high taxes of beach property and the corrosive effects of the salt air. On the return trip, in south Georgia, George had consulted his map and turned off the interstate several times to explore remote roads. He returned to Atlanta satisfied that he had found just what he had been seeking.

George studied the computer printout, shielding the flashlight with his hand. He scanned down the fan-folded pages. His eyes lingered on several lines: obtain sleep medication from Margaret's prescription, prepare coffee, pour contents of sleep medication capsules into blue Thermos ...walk through inspection to determine house is ready for new owners, assure all doors, windows locked ...depart home six in evening, maintain 55 mph, exit I-275 onto I-75 South... stop for evening meal at Shoney's 63.7 miles from point of departure, order all-you-can-eat fish (most nutritious for cost) ...Exit I-75 at Ga. exit No. 4 (Valdosta), Ga. Hwy. 94 18.6 miles to river. His finger traced to the bottom. Next entries: discard shovel; discard blue Thermos.

He folded the shovel and tightened the threaded nut to hold it in folded position, walked to the center of the narrow bridge beside which he had parked, and flung the shovel downstream. He opened the blue Thermos, poured the remaining tainted coffee into the river, pounded the bottle against the rusted steel handrail until he heard the glass liner shatter, and threw it into the water.

He slid into the driver's seat and closed the door all but a couple of inches. He slipped a finger between the door and the front sill, peeled a 2"x2" piece of duct tape from the push-pull switch for the dome light, quickly jerked his fingers out of the space and pulled the door closed. That entry was checked off. He rolled the piece of tape into a tiny ball and tossed it out the window as he drove across the bridge.

Just before he completed the 18.6 mile drive back to the interstate, he drove slowly, careful not to violate any traffic laws. On his way to the river he had noticed a small store front with GOODWILL lettered in crude gothic on the window, and a large, soiled wooden box in front. He pulled close to the box, opened the trunk, took Margaret's clothes from her suitcases and pushed them through the opening into the big box. He put her few items of jewelry into a small plastic bag and pushed it into the space next to the spare tire. Two more check marks were made on the printout.

As he drove toward the Florida state line, he thought about the past few hours. Things had gone according to plan except for their being three-and-a-half minutes late leaving home. He had been in the car waiting to start the engine until Margaret was in the car. He blew the horn impatiently and tapped the steering wheel with his fingers as he waited. "Well, I had to take one last look around the house, and I had to get the coffee," Margaret explained as she maneuvered her bulk, a purse, two Thermos bottles, a bag of cheese puffs (stuffed halfway under her light sweater, because George did not like anyone to eat or smoke in the car), and a box of tissues into the seat. "I don't understand why we have to travel at night, I get so sleepy when we travel at night."

She struggled with the seat belt as the car engine warmed up for exactly thirty seconds before George shifted into reverse. "I know, I know, the highway is less crowded, and it's cooler so there's less wear on the tires, and we don't have to use the air conditioner after seven ...whatever ..forty five."

"Six fifteen."

Margaret's struggles with the seat belt while juggling the thermos bottles, tissues and corn puffs caused her purse to slide off her lap and dump half its contents on the floor.

"My plan called for us to leave three and a half minutes ago," George grumbled as he checked the fuel and the oil pressure gauges and the inside and outside mirrors.

"Plan, plan, plan. George, let's just go."

"You don't appreciate the value of proper planning..."

"Oh, yes, George, I do, I do. Months ago I told you I had a plan all written out. I still do."

"A plan is no good unless it is implemented."

"I'm going to implement it, George. Soon. Believe me. Very soon," Margaret responded as she bent over to find all the odds-and-ends that had fallen from her purse.

She put the two Thermos bottles they always carried on trips into the holder George had designed, George's red Thermos with black coffee next to him, Margaret's blue one filled with coffee with cream and sugar on her side... the blue thermos with coffee, cream, sugar, and the contents of one hundred twenty-three of Margaret's Nembutal capsules that had done their job perfectly, just as he had planned.

For some time, George had periodically slipped a few from the prescription bottle Margaret kept on her bedside table. As he had anticipated, Margaret had seemed oblivious to the fact that it had been necessary to refill her prescription for one hundred of the capsules after she had taken only seventy-five or so. George knew that she never kept track of such things the way he did.

Margaret had stayed awake until they stopped for dinner. The meal, the monotony of the interstate, the constant hum of the tires, and the increase in temperature after George had turned off the air conditioner at six-fifteen had lulled her to sleep.

After dark, George had flipped on the air conditioner for a few seconds, then turned it off. The blast of cold air had roused Margaret.

"Oh, goodness," she said as she took off her glasses and rubbed her eyes, "I didn't intend to fall asleep. I guess a little coffee would help keep me awake." She poured a portion into the top to the blue thermos, took a swallow and made a face. "Strong," she said, "kind of bitter. It's all right. After another cup of this, I'll be ready to drive all night. I know, I know, constant fifty-five, check the gauges, fill up at a quarter of a tank." She poured more coffee and drank it.

An hour later she was slumped in the seat. Her breathing had become labored. Twice, she had made noises as though she was gagging or gasping for breath. Then she made no sound. George reached across the seat and pressed his fingers against her neck to check the carotid artery for a pulse. His hand shook so that he had to check three times to be sure there was no pulse.

Three-and-a-half minutes behind schedule, the three and-a-half minutes lost when Margaret had been late getting into the car, George thought as he crossed the Florida State line. He had taken the gloves out of the trunk and thrown one onto the Interstate, the other twenty-three miles later, knowing that they could never be traced to him, especially after they had been run over by several hundred cars. He had decided to keep the rubber boots. They were clean from his wading in the river, they were expensive, and they had been worn only once.

Twice he had stopped, once for gasoline and to discard the sheets of plastic in the station's dumpster, and once a short distance down a side road where he dumped Margaret's suitcases and purse in the woods after burning anything with Margaret's name and address, and throwing her cosmetics and other odds-and-ends into a gopher hole. By the light of the burning papers, he had checked and double checked the computer printout, made one final check, reluctantly laid it on the small fire and watched it burn.

As he drove he smiled to himself, satisfied that he had developed and carried out a perfect, detailed, viable plan, and happy with his thoughts of a future where everything would be meticulously planned; where there would be no wasted time or money. A place for everything - everything in its place. He would enjoy a life in which the last hour before bedtime each evening would be devoted to preparing a detailed plan for the following day.

It was past midnight. He was very tired from driving, from the stress of carrying out his perfect plan, and from the unaccustomed physical exertion. He slowed the car to exactly fifty miles an hour and poured a cup of coffee from the red Thermos.

* * * * *

The deputy sat across the desk from the Sheriff and unfolded a sheet of paper. "This is the coroner's report you asked about. Franklin. From Atlanta. Subject apparently overdosed on barbituates. Probably sleeping pills."

The Sheriff frowned and leaned forward, his interest piqued. "What about notification of next of kin?"

"Evidently, there are no children, and the Atlanta Police haven't been able to find any relatives so far. They have found out that Mrs. Franklin left Atlanta last Monday evening with Mr. Franklin. He retired a year or so ago. They sold their house and were moving to somewhere near the coast. Nobody seemed to know exactly where."

"Anything else?"

"There was some jewelry--nothing really expensive--in a plastic bag jammed between the spare tire and the side of the spare tire well. And we found a smashed, red Thermos with traces of black coffee loaded with a barbituate. Mr. Franklin wouldn't have put sleeping pills in his own coffee. So, I think we should start looking for Mrs. Franklin. She was in the car when they left Atlanta, but wasn't in it when it wrecked. Mr. Franklin may have been dead when it hit the overpass abutment-- or asleep."

The deputy passed a wrinkled scrap of lined yellow paper torn from a pad to the Sheriff. "This was found under the passenger side of the front seat."

The Sheriff smoothed the paper and read the three words scrawled on it in feminine handwriting:

PLAN
KILL GEORGE

Old Tom and Twinkleberry

Old Tom was a fighter and a lover, not necessarily in that order of preference, but the two always seemed to go together. He would watch over things that went on about our farm and then, whenever he felt that we could carry on without him for a while, he would quietly pad off in the dark of night to make his rounds of the other farms in the area, bestowing his "favors" on the she cats he could seduce with wile and charm.

At home, Old Tom was a gentle, lovable fellow who patiently endured the humiliation of being dressed in outgrown baby clothes by my brother Charlie and me. And he enjoyed walking along the top rail of our small corral while Jerry, the white-faced-Hereford steer, licked him head to tail with one sweep of a tongue while Tom held on with all twenty claws to keep from being slurped off the fence. "

During his frequent romantic forays, which sometimes extended into two or three days and nights, he was like an old-time gunslinger who was willing to fight for what he thought was rightfully his, the results of which were well documented in the form of fringed ears, multiple scars, and an eye blinded by another he cat who insisted on protecting his own territory from this big orange-and-red -striped threat.

In spite of his frequent amorous wanderings, his true love was Twinkleberry, a sleek, multicolored, tortoise shell who lived with Miss Tillery, the little, silver-haired old maid whose two acres bordered our twenty on the north. Miss Tillery doted on Twinkleberry and fed her cooked, chopped liver and kidney with a side serving of dry Puffed Wheat washed down with a saucer of cream skimmed from the quart mason jars of milk that I delivered to her twice a week for twenty cents each.

Old Tom was drowsing in the sun on the front porch when something, unheard by us, suddenly attracted his attention. He raised his head and looked straight at Miss Tillery's/Twinkleberry's house. His ears went straight up, and his single pupil went so big one could hardly see the bright yellow-green that surrounded it. He took no time to stretch the kinks from his muscles, as was his usual habit, but bounded off the porch and headed straight toward the home of his true love. Minutes later, as he squeezed through the fence, he saw Twinkleberry sitting in the middle of Miss Tillery's bed of monkey-faced pansies coyly eyeing a young, handsome, black and white suitor partly hidden behind a four-o'clock bush. Old Tom sat down in the dirt driveway behind Miss Tillery's Model "T" Ford and studied the situation with his one good eye.

Twinkleberry looked at Old Tom and then at the young fellow who had strutted down the two-rut sand road from the Junkin's place and then back at Old Tom and then back at the younger fellow, apparently considering that perhaps the younger one, with his lean, muscular build and smooth coat was a little more appealing than Old Tom with his heavy frame, legs as sturdy as those on Miss Tillery's mahogany dining table, a head as big as two of Grandma's "cat head" biscuits, fringed ears, multiple scars and only one eye with which to admire her.

The young fellow made some derogatory comment about Old Tom while aloofly licking a paw, and Old Tom felt compelled to reply in kind. The young fellow halted in the middle of a lick and looked at Old Tom and said something that Old Tom didn't like. The threats, name-calling and challenges began to be exchanged in earnest, becoming louder and shriller. Twinkleberry sat between them in the middle of Miss Tillery's bed of monkey-faced pansies and looked, wide-eyed, back and forth, from one to the other.

The young fellow made some comment concerning Old Tom's age and ability to fight, and Old Tom was on him in a flash. The name-calling became ear-shattering and there was a mighty tangle of legs and bodies with clashing teeth and slashing claws. The two tumbled and rolled in the dirt and made so much noise they woke Miss Tillery from her afternoon nap, and Twinkleberry sat in the middle of the bed of monkey-faced pansies, frightened, but, at the same time, kind of flattered that the two were fighting over her.

The fight was vicious, but short-lived. The young fellow suddenly decided that it was time to go home to the Junkin's place, and took off down the two-rut sand road with Old Tom right behind, raking the young fellow's fanny with his claws on every third or fourth step until the young fellow was well clear of Miss Tillery's yard.

Old Tom stopped and sat in the middle of the two-rut sand road for a few minutes, watching the young black-and-white until he was out of sight, and then went back and sat beside Twinkleberry in the middle of Miss Tillery's bed of monkey-faced pansies and Twinkleberry gave her hero a loving lick on a fringed ear.

The young fellow slowed as he got to the turnoff into the Junkin's place, suddenly conscious of the pains of a chewed ear, three claw furrows across his nose, numerous scratches on his fanny, and the cat equivalent of a Charlie horse in his left hind leg, but his pride wouldn't permit him to admit his defeat to the several she cats who lived at the Junkin's place.

He called them all into the barn and, strutting as best he could, told them of how he had challenged the legendary Old Tom, and that Old Tom wasn't nearly as tough as all the other cats had said, and how *he* had given Old Tom the thrashing of his life, and that Old Tom wasn't near the cat *he* was.

The she cats sat solemn-faced and listened to his bragging with nods and grunts. When he had run out of pronouncements, he went outside so his sore muscles could soak up the warm sunshine.

The she cats sat in sort of a circle, like prim little ladies at a quilting bee, and looked about at their many orange-and-red striped progeny who, with their heavy frames, sturdy legs like Miss Tillery's mahogany table, and heads already nearly as big as one of Grandma's "cat head" biscuits, chased and leaped and stalked imaginary mice. The she cats looked around at one another and smiled.

MORE POEMS

Epitaph

Here lies a cheating gambler named Joe
Drew aces too fast—his gun too slow

Cinquian

Fall wind
Steals crimson leaves
And spreads them on the ground
As a carpet for the great king
Winter.

Haiku

The cattails glory
Browns and flies like tiny wrens
Away on soft breeze

Mrs. Bailey's Butterbeans

Mrs. Irma Bailey heard the car when it turned off the hard road nearly a mile away. She knew from its sound that it didn't belong to one of the families who lived on the neighboring farms, and it wasn't the mailman. His car made a lower, louder sound.

Mrs. Bailey lifted the skirt of her light cotton dress that hung nearly to her ankles ...nearly to the top of her high-top, pointed-toed shoes-and went to the living room window. She squinted out, then took her round, gold-rimmed spectacles from her apron pocket, hooked the bows over her ears and adjusted them on her nose with a push of a forefinger. As she leaned over, looking out the window for the intruder into the morning quiet, she took a curved tortoise-shell comb from the back of her head, palmed wisps of silver upward from her nape and anchored them in place by pushing the comb back into the base of the tightly wound bun at the back of her head.

She heard the car slowing before she could see it, her view blocked by scrub pines and haw apple trees that had sprung up in the six years since the south ten acres had been farmed. Six years since Edward had left.

She stepped back from the window and pulled the lace curtains together in a single movement when the car appeared, turned into the sand driveway and stopped behind her 1924 Model "T" Touring car.

"Oh my goodness," Mrs. Bailey mumbled, "Now who on earth could that be?" She forefingered her glasses into position again and tried squinting to clear her view thorough the lace.

The driver got out and walked around the front of the car. He was young - to her he was young - maybe thirty or thirty-five, short and on the heavy side. Red faced. White shirt with sleeves rolled to the elbows, blue tie loosely knotted, gray seersucker pants, black suspenders, and a summer Panama hat. He stopped and wiped his face with his handkerchief, then walked up the two steps to the porch of the small frame house.

He stepped to the door and poked his head out trying to see into the front room, blinded against the dark inside by the bright sun reflected off the sand road. "Oooh hooo, Miz. Bailey, oooh hooo," he cooed as he tapped lightly on the door facing as though worried that he might bruise his freckled knuckles.

Mrs. Bailey pulled at her skirt, adjusted her faded blue apron, and fingered her glasses into place again. She went to the door and, through habit, placed her finger on the small wire hook that tentatively locked the wood-framed screen door. "Yes?" she asked.

The man took off his Panama hat and held it over his heart. "Mrs. Bailey, I'm Buford Harris. I'm garden and flower editor for the Tribune(?)," he said in an alto that climbed to a higher note at the end of the statement to turn it into a pseudo-query. "My sister, Eileen Purdom, is the home demonstration agent.(?) Well, she had me over to her house for supper last Sunday evening before church and she served a bowl of the biggest, most scrumptious butter beans that I have ever put in my mouth." This time his voice lowered to a tone that denoted some degree of ecstasy and his eyes rolled toward heaven. "Well, I asked where in the world she got those wonderful butter beans, and she told me that you had given them to her. That you grew the biggest and best butter beans of anybody around. And she said your butter bean vines are the lushest she has ever seen." He closed his eyes for a moment, then opened them wider than before. "Well, to make a long story short, I felt that I simply had to come out to see you and, with your permission, devote next week's column to your butter beans."

Mrs. Bailey moved her finger and lifted the hook from the metal eye screwed into the door facing. "Goodness, I don't know why anybody would want to make a fuss over my butter beans ...they're just butter beans," she said as she stepped out the door onto the porch. "Nothing to really make a fuss over. They are good beans, I'll have to admit that, but I declare, I never expected anybody to ever write about them in the newspaper. Just follow me on around back and I'll show you my butter beans. "Don't know why anybody would want to write about them."

She stepped off the porch and walked briskly past Buford Harris's car and her twelve-year-old Model "T" with Buford Harris following close behind, wiping his face with his handkerchief before putting on his hat to protect his scalp from the sun rays searing their way through his sparse hair that was combed from lower left across the top of his head.

Behind the house was the typical kitchen garden: cabbage, carrots, green beans, turnips, radishes, a couple rows of each and four rows of corn, the edges of the long leaves laced by hungry caterpillars.

But to the left, beside the small, weathered garage, was Mrs. Bailey's butter bean patch. It was a small patch, maybe seven or eight feet long and three or four feet wide, with a trellis of slim tree branches leaned against the edge of the garage roof and stout cordage woven back and forth among the poles.

The vines were truly lush. The stalks were twice as sturdy as the average butter bean plant. They had to be to support the array of runners that covered the length of the trellis and then some, climbed to the roof and crept like long, searching fingers halfway up the roof. And the bean pods. Such pods. Pods eight, ten inches long pregnant with fat, juicy beans.

Buford Harris's eyes bulged as he took off his hat, held it over his heart, and stood quietly in a moment of reverence. "My word," he whispered, "I have never, ever in my life seen such butterbean vines. They're beautiful. Simply beautiful." He put on his hat and walked softly to the plants, looked them up and down and from side to side and gently touched a few of the leaves and pods.

He took a note pad and a yellow pencil with a metal clip and a push-on two-for-a-penny eraser from his shirt pocket. He licked the point of the pencil and flipped back the cover and a few pages of the pad. "How long have you been growing butter beans in this particular spot, Mrs. Bailey?"

"Let me see, six years, yes, six years. Just after we moved here from Jacksonville. We had a business of our own in Jacksonville. We moved here for the good of Edward's health. Edward was my husband, my dear, departed husband." She took a filmy, lace-edged hanky from her pocket and dabbed at her eyes and nose.

"Butterbeans were his favorite, such a good man, and they were his favorite."

Buford stared at the tiny lady standing beside him for a moment, a look of consolation on his face. "How long has Edwar...Mr. Bailey been gone, Mrs. Bailey?"

"Nearly six years. Very soon after we moved here in nineteen thirty. None of the neighbors ever got to know him. He was here, and then... She dabbed again.

"Mrs. Bailey, what is your secret for growing such magnificent butter beans? Do you use any special fertilizer?"

"Oh no, just a little of the ...uh...material from the floor of the chicken coop now and then. Nothing special. Just a good spot for butter beans, I suppose. George and Robert loved them, too."

"George and Robert?"

"Our two sons. They loved butter beans, too. But George is living up north now and Robert...poor Robert passed on at an early age - so young - only twenty-two, just after his daddy, Edward. Such wonderful children." She looked up at Buford.

Buford took off his hat, tried to juggle the hat, a note pad and his pencil, then put the hat back on. "What in heaven do you do with all those beans, Mrs. Bailey?"

"Oh, I put some of them up in Mason Jars, and I dry some for cooking and for seed, and I give some to my special friends. Would you like some Mr ....?

"Harris. Please, call me Buford. Oh, I would love to have some. If you can spare a few." He rolled his eyes heavenward. "Yes."

"Oh, tish, there's plenty. Let me get a grocery sack and we'll pick some for you." She started toward the kitchen door.

"While you're getting a sack, I'll get my camera from the car. I hope you don't mind if I take your picture in front of those magnificent butter bean vines."

Irma Bailey stopped and thought for a moment, then turned and looked at Buford. "No, it'll be all right. I don't mind." She went on toward the kitchen. "Just don't know why anybody wants to make a fuss over a few butter beans."

Together they picked three-fourths of a sack full of beans, and there was no obvious dwindling in the number of pods hanging heavy on the vines. Mrs. Bailey showed Buford how she hooked the high-growing runners with a hoe to pull them low enough for her to pick the pods. As they picked, Buford Harris asked more questions about the beans and how she grew them. Occasionally, he would take out his pad and pencil and make a few notes.

Buford rolled the top of the sack and put it in the shade. "Now Mrs. Bailey, if you'll stand about here, facing the sun, I'll take a couple of snapshots for the paper.(?) No, no, don't put the hoe down. Pretend you're using it.(?) Please forgive me, but I'll need to take several, because I'm forever getting my thumb in the way or jiggling the camera or something."

He took eight pictures, fidgeting with the box camera between snaps. Irma Bailey shaded her eyes while he fidgeted and she grew hotter and less patient.

"Mrs. Bailey, I do appreciate your taking your time to talk to me and letting me take your picture, and for those wonderful butter beans," Buford Harris said as he slid onto the hot front seat of his car. "I'll try to get your story in this week's paper.(?) If I can't make it this week... I've been so busy... it will surely be in next week's." He looked at Irma Bailey for a few seconds, then said softly, "You are such a dear, dear lady," closing his eyes for a couple of beats on the second dear.

As he drove away down the sand road, Buford leaned across the seat toward the passenger door and wiggled his fingers as a good bye to Irma. Irma pulled the lace-edged, filmy hanky from the pocket of her apron and waved it at the departing car.

Irma Bailey stuffed the hanky into her pocket. Still carrying the hoe, she walked back to the butter bean patch. She swung the hoe hard and true, chopping off the tiny, double leaves of a weed that had poked up through the sandy soil.

"Dear, departed Edward. He was such a good man," she said in a high pitched, mocking voice as she waggled her head from side to side. "Worthless sonofabitch! Moved here because of his health. A dozen people in Jacksonville wanted to kill him."

"Such a good man. We had our own business. Sonofabitch drank and gambled away our money and our business. Only way we got the money for this worthless place was by him making a killing on some illegal liquor from the Bahamas."

Irma chopped with the hoe again. "George and Robert. Such wonderful children. George lives up north now. About eighty miles north in Raiford prison for the rest of his life for shooting his girlfriend's husband. And that no good Robert died so young along with the Junkins boy from drinking bootleg they made using a car radiator for an evaporator."

"Edward. Worthless sonofabitch couldn't do anything right. Drank, gambled, beat the kids. Hit me one time. Just one time." She hacked again with the hoe, harder.

"He couldn't do anything right by himself, and we couldn't do anything right together. Not even raise kids."

Irma Bailey stopped and looked at the butter bean vines that sprawled across the trellis and climbed halfway up the roof of the garage. "Well, I guess there is one thing." She leaned over, looked at the soft earth of the bean patch and tamped it a couple of times with the flat head of the hoe. "We do grow a pretty fair crop of butter beans together, don't we Edward?"

A FEW MORE POEMS

Tonka

White sails full of wind
Pushing my boat across seas
Toward strange new lands
No salt spray splashes my face
My travels: words from a book.

Triolet

Yep, I knew ol' Moody Cass
But we wuz never really friends
We drank and hunted and fished for bass
Yep, I knew ol' Moody Cass
We ate together at the diner
We cut each other's grass
I ain't goin' to his funeral
Here's where it ends
Yep, I knew ol' Moody Cass
But we waz never really friends

The Black Box

He wiped a thin layer of dust off the top of the small, black lacquered box and tilted his head back to bring his bifocals into focus so that he could read the words painted on the lid.

George thought of the things that his nephew, David, had said and how he had used the same words over and over,

"Uncle George, you'd never believe."

He brushed his fingers through his thin, graying hair. "David," he said, "you'd never believe...".

David, his brother's son, had dropped by unexpectedly that evening. He had rung the front door bell just as George was finishing his lonely dinner in front of the television, the same type lonely dinner he had eaten in front of the television for the past four years. No need to use the dining room and maybe mess up the antique walnut table he had bought for Margret so many years ago.

George hadn't recognized David at first. He hadn't seen him in nearly fifteen years and David had changed so much; heavier, bigger, his hair shorter ...much shorter. Older now. A man, not a boy anymore.

"I was passing through and thought I would look you up," David had said. They shook hands and hugged each other kind of quick and not too close, the way men do with somebody they should hug close, but haven't seen for a while.

They had talked about family and about the work David was doing these days and David had said how sorry he had been when he had heard about Aunt Margret.

And David told his Uncle George what it had been like and how rough it had been to be a "grunt", a slogging, dog face ...a foot soldier of the Infantry.

"Uncle George, you'd never believe how it was to see one of your good buddies shot and die right beside you. Uncle George, you'd never believe how it was to have one of your squad blown to bits by a land mine or a mortar round. Uncle George, you'd never believe how hot it was. Uncle George, you'd never believe how bad you can feel when you see women and children who were killed by rocket fire or napalm from a jet. Uncle George, you'd never believe how it hurts to get shot."

And "Uncle George, you'd never believe how bad"it feels to know that you've left behind over a thousand MIA"s."

George got beer from the refrigerator for the two of them while David kept telling him how good it was to see him and how that he'd never believe how bad it was to be in combat.

After an hour-and-a-half David told George again how good it had been to see him and how good it was to talk to him and how they shouldn't wait so long to see each other again.

George waved goodbye closed the door and locked it.

He tugged his worn-elbow cardigan closer and stopped at the thermostat to boost the temperature a few degrees.

He settled into his comfortably-broken-in chair, kicked off his slippers and put his heels into the two matching dips worn into the top of the hassock.

For the next twenty minutes he looked at the television. He looked at it, but he didn't watch what was on the screen. He looked and he thought. He thought about David's words, and he thought about his own buddies.

He padded in sock feet to the bedroom and knelt in front of the chest of drawers that was still crammed with socks and underwear and sweaters and odds and ends. He had not yet been able to bring himself to clean out the dresser Margret's dresser - and use it for his own things, so his chest of drawers was still crammed full.

The bottom drawer - the one filled with odds and ends- stuck a little, so it took a couple of tugs before it slid open. He took out some things and pushed aside some others, and then he lifted out a small, black lacquered box.

He wiped a thin layer of dust off the top of the small, black lacquered box and tilted his head back to bring his bifocals into focus so that he could see better what was painted on the lid.

There was a map of a country far away from here, but not so far from Viet Nam. Small dots of mother-of-pearl were inlaid to indicate the location of cities with strange names like Pusan, Seoul, Potsung, Kunsan, and Inchon. The smallest key on his chain he used to unlock the tiny lock.

George took the contents out of the box, a roll of dark blue velvet and two newspaper clippings. He read one of the clippings about the Korean War memorial in Washington, D. C....finally, after so many years.

The second clipping was older and yellowed. It told about casualties during the Korean "Police Action," More than thirty-nine thousand Americans killed, 103,248 wounded and 5,178 left behind as missing in action.

He unrolled the dark blue velvet, smoothed it on the top of the chest of drawers, and looked at the medals pinned to it. The Korean Service medal with three stars for major battles, The United Nations Medal, The Purple Heart with cluster-- twice wounded --two Purple Hearts, The Bronze Star with two clusters, a blue bar with silver rifle and wreath... The Combat Infantry Badge, Unit Citations, The Syngman Rhee Medal of Gallentry from the Republic of South Korea, and the collar brass with crossed muskets -- the insignia of the infantry... the foot-slogging dog face, foot soldier.

As he touched each one he thought about his buddies who had been blown to bits, about the Marines who froze to death at the Chosin Reservoir, about the women and children who died by rocket fire or napalm from jets. He thought about how bad it was to be in combat and how it hurts to be shot.

He looked at the map on the lid, brushed his fingers through his thin, graying hair. "David," he said, "you'd never believe ...."

George rolled up the piece of velvet and put it and the newspaper clippings back in the box, locked it and slipped it back where he felt such memories should be: locked away in a black box at the back of the bottom drawer.

My Criminal Past

I was astonished by the news report. The crime occurred a couple of weeks ago. A boy kissed a classmate on the cheek. He was expelled from school. The charge: sexual harassment.

Expelled? Sexual harassment? Will he have a police record? Will parents keep their children from playing with him? Will they demand that he and his family move out of the neighborhood?

The questions made my skin crawl. The possible answers made me break out in a cold sweat. Why? Because the situation brought back recollections of my own sordid past.

Memories jarred my brain. I thought of hiding in the back room ...or shaving my beard and mustache, letting my hair grow and dying it black so that nobody would recognize me. The authorities wouldn't be able to find me. Long moments of terror--then cooler thoughts prevailed. Maybe, after seventy-five years, the statute of limitations...

But I feel the need to confess--to come clean--to get it off my chest. Yes, I did it; And I was his age when I did it.

Six.

She had olive complexion, brown hair with reddish overtones, and dark brown eyes. She was tall (for a six year old), and she could outrun every boy in the first grade--not that she had to, she just liked to race them, and beat them.

We were in Mean Old Miz Johnson's class on the second floor of the Ocala Primary School. (That was back in the days when school authorities considered first graders old enough to traverse a flight of stairs ...the thought of a million dollar lawsuit resulting from a skinned knee never entered their minds).

Mean Old Miz Johnson was at least a hundred years old and certainly posed for Halloween posters. She was as thin as a tether ball post. Her hair, white as chalk, was pulled back severely and knotted into a tight bun held in place with long ivory skewers. Her icy blue eyes could pierce the armor of the bravest student, and few were the boys whose knuckles escaped the lightning fast raps of her ever-present steel-edged ruler. Mine escaped until Frank dropped a gaggle of marbles that clattered on the floor, and he told her they were mine.

I had waited as long as I could before timidly raising my hand and pointing my index finger toward the big globular lights that hung by chains from the ceiling. After an eternity those icy eyes focused on mine. It was a long, long moment before she gave a nearly imperceptible nod. I slipped from my desk, tiptoed to the door, opened it just enough to slip through, and closed it as quietly as my haste and the weight of the heavy door would permit. I walked as fast as I dared toward the wide stairs. The only rest rooms were downstairs ...out back... in a separate little building that I suspect had begun its existence as a double-sided, multi-holed privy. I started down the stairs, reaching up to hold on to the heavy wooden balustrade worn shiny smooth over decades by thousands of small hands.

Then I saw her below me, starting up the stairs. At the halfway mark--being the gentleman Mom had taught me to be- -I stepped aside for her to pass. Instead of passing, she stopped. I stopped. She said nothing; she just leaned over and gave me a warm, soft, lingering kiss... full on the lips. Still, she said nothing, just continued her way to the second floor and Mean Old Miz Johnson's room. I stood there watching her climbing those wide steps, touching the heavy, shiny, wooden balustrade until a pang reminded me why I had raised my hand and pointed a finger toward the ceiling.

At recess I was still dazed. My heart wasn't into playing tag, or dodge ball. I just sat idly on the low end of a seesaw, periodically bumping the wide plank hard on the ground while Frank clung to the high end and screamed for me to let him down. When it was time for us to line up to go back to the classroom (boys in one line, girls in another) I saw her walking toward me. She smiled. She was beautiful ...even with two front teeth missing.

"Whenever I go to the bathroom," she said, "wait a few minutes and raise your hand. I'll meet you on the stairs."

Later that afternoon she raised her hand. She looked at me and smiled as she passed my desk.

So began romance on the stairs. It didn't happen every day, or even every week, but it happened often enough that I am sure Mean Old Miz Johnson knew there was cause for our bladders becoming synchronized. The principal must have known. Her office was on the first floor just across the hall from the stairs. They probably talked it over and laughed at the harmless flirtations of two six-year-olds.

Everyone remembers their first kiss and where and when it happened: on the porch swing, in a dark corner while playing hide and seek, a game of post office, or spin the bottle, or on the wide stairs with the shiny wooden balustrade in Primary School in 1936. And they never forget the person who shared that kiss.

Her name was Rose.

Golden Anniversary

1934

"Me and Eddie and Pauline and Charlene and Jack want to do somethin' special for you two. It's fittin' for the children to do somethin' special for their Ma and Pa when they been married for fifty years. They call that the Golden anniversary and we figure it'll be fifty years next month that you two been married. You ain't never made any fuss over your anniversaries, but we know it's sometime in June and we want to give a party for you." Robert Starling sat backward in the cane-bottomed chair, his forearms resting on the top of the back, and looked at his parents sitting across the dining table eating their Saturday farm supper of turnip greens and corn bread left to stay warm on the back of the wood-burning stove, and jelly glasses of buttermilk from a quart Mason jar set in a heavy crock filled with cool pump water and covered with a damp cloth.

Robert, like his father across the table, wore hard work and boiling pot-faded bib overalls and a long-sleeved cotton work shirt that was buttoned to the collar, common outfits for Florida dirt farmers during the thirties…durable clothing for hard work and protection from the scorching sun.

Adrian Starling was a small man, tough as hog wire, who appeared even smaller since his shoulders had rounded with the years and his thin blond hair had aged to shiny white.

Ruby Starling fingered the straps of her home made cotton-print apron, and then fidgeted with the curved comb that held the bun of nearly white hair at her nape. Her hands were tanned from hoeing in her kitchen garden, and, though lumpy from arthritis, were still supple enough to embroider pretties for her daughters and grandchildren. "No use in makin' no fuss over it this time, neither. It's just another year and…"

"Don't need no party. Never liked get-togethers. Whole lot of bother for nothin'." Adrian Starling interrupted his wife. "Fifty ain't no different from forty or thirty or twenty. Just ain't got as many to go as we been through, that's all. Ain't even sure it's been fifty years. Might be forty eight or nine. Don't remember." He didn't look up from his plate as he talked, then scooped up a forkful of greens and bit off a corner of cornbread generously soaked with pot liquor, punctuating the end of his speech with a flourish of food on his fork.

Robert looked at his father. "You and Ma always said you got married in June of 1886. This is nineteen thirty-six and that makes fifty years. This is gonna be your golden anniversary. We want to do somethin' special. Besides, you always seemed to like get-togethers. I've seen you clapping your hands and doin' that dance of yours when Mose Jordan scraped the fiddle and Mister Mulkey played the guitar and Bully Martin plunked on that old banjo." He leaned forward against the back of the chair and moved his hands to grip the sides of the back. "I plum don't understand why you don't want no party."

Adrian looked across the table at his wife who was adjusting the combs at the back of her head again. He slowly put his fork down across his plate, wiped his mouth on the back of his hand, and turned partly toward Robert, but looked down as though afraid, or ashamed to meet the eyes of his son. He hesitated, pondering over the right words to use. It was difficult for him to tell his son something that he and Ruby had kept secret for so many years.

"Can't have no party 'cause there ain't going to be no anniversary," Adrian said slowly, choosing his words. "There ain't going to be no fiftieth or fifty-first or fifty-second. Ain't going to be none and there ain't never been none. Never told you and the others 'cause we didn't want you all to be ashamed of us 'cause we ain't never got married official like in front of a preacher or a Justice of the Peace or nobody."

"You ain't really married?"

"No, we didn't have a regular preacher where we was livin' in Tennessee, just a circuit rider name of Beaudry that came around every month or so and held a service, baptized babies, married young folks and prayed over the graves of anybody that had died since he'd been around last."

"Couldn't he have married you?"

"We was plannin' for him to marry us, but he got drowned," Ruby Starling said.

Adrian took a drink of buttermilk and wiped his mouth. "Durn fool preacher never could ride too good. Tried to ride that old mare of his across White Water Creek after a week of heavy rain. Guess the mare stepped in a hole and Preacher Beaudry fell off and. drowned. The mare wandered up to the little settlement where we lived. Saddle bags was full of water so we figured what had happened. Some folks that lived a couple miles down the creek found the preacher's body a couple days later."

"Didn't somebody take his place?"

"Well, somebody did after a while. Name was Wiggins... Wig..."

"Wilkinson," Ruby Starling said.

"Wilkinson. Yeah, name was Wilkinson. But it was nearly a year before he came around, and your ma and me, we got tired of waitin' so we took the Bible that was in Preacher Beaudry's saddlebag and we helt it together between us and we both said we took the other one and said I do and told everbody that we was married. We was goin' to let the new preacher Wigg..Wi..."

"Wilkinson."

"Wilkinson. Hell, I know it, woman! Anyway, we was gonna let that preacher make it official when he came around, but, like I said, it was nearly a year and by that time your mother was plumb out to here in the family way... just about ready to have you... and we was kind of ashamed to let him know that we never got married official like with her in that condition. When we moved down here your brother Eddie was on the way, and…well, one thing after another come up and we just never found the right time to ask anybody to marry us official like. After a while we couldn't do it with all you kids. And that's why we can't have no golden anniversary party. Wouldn't be right."

Robert leaned down, slid his dollar straw hat out from under the chair and stood up. He held the hat over his heart with both hands and looked at his mother and father without expression. "No, I don't suppose it would be right to have a golden wedding anniversary party if there ain't never been no wedding. I'll-I'll go tell the others." He turned and walked out of the house without looking back, the slap of the screen door closing behind him announcing finality to the conversation.

A week passed without Adrian and Ruby Starling seeing Robert or any of their other children. They all lived close by with their own families and it had been a rare day that one of them or one of the older grandchildren didn't come to see them or drop by for a minute on their way somewhere. Adrian Starling had a strange, sick feeling inside, brought on by the belief that by telling the truth he and Ruby had lost the love and respect of their family, that their children were too embarrassed to even come see them any more. He had started to talk to Ruby about it several times, but he never seemed to be able to get the right words out.

Adrian and Ruby sat at the dining table eating their light supper, having had their heavier meal in the middle of the day when Adrian had taken a couple of hours off from his work in the fields, a respite from the heat and work that continued until near dark. The two didn't talk much, Adrian commented on how well the watermelons, his main crop that year, were coming along and Ruby told Adrian that she needed more stakes and string for the peas that grew in her kitchen garden that flourished conveniently near the back door.

Adrian swallowed a chunk of biscuit, then stopped and listened for the sound he had just heard. "Hear that?" he asked Ruby. "Sounds like a car...maybe two...comin' down the road...and a bunch of people jabbering. Ain't normal for folks to be comin' down the road this time of night."

Ruby pushed back her chair and went and swung open the screen door. She stepped out on the porch and looked down the road. "I believe you're right," she said. "Looks like a lot of folks coming down the road."

Adrian walked past her and out into the front yard. He looked down the two-rut dirt road. "There's a wagon load of people...looks like Moody Cass's wagon...and a couple of cars. Some folks ridin' horses, too." By the time he got the words out of his mouth the wagon pulled by a team of matched mules had turned into the yard followed by an almost new Model "A" Ford driven by somebody Adrian didn't recognize and Miss Tillery's 1924 Model "T" touring car. The wagon and the two cars were loaded with people, members of the Starling family and friends they had known for years. There was old man Junkins and his young, redheaded wife, Ned and Irene Mulkey and Bully Martin and Mose Jordan, the Krazits, the Hesters. Robert Starling alighted from the passenger door of the Model "A" and walked around to the driver's door. The driver, a heavy-set young man wearing a black suit and a black felt hat, got out and the two talked for a time.

"Who in the world is that?" Ruby whispered.

"I don't know...maybe a judge, wearing that black suit," Adrian said softly.

"Everybody looks so serious. I wonder what they want."

"Oh, good Lord. Robert's done told everbody that we ain't married and all them Baptists have come out here to run us off. They don't take to unholy things like that, you know. And that judge is goin' to charge us with adulterry...or forn...forni...or what ever it is he can charge us with! I never figured Robert and the others would take this so hard...shouldn't a told him." Robert and the man in black walked to the front steps and faced Adrian and Ruby. "Ma, Pa," Robert said, "this here is Reverend Jody Lee. He's the preacher at the Baptist Church in Anthony. He wants to talk to you."

Adrian swallowed hard. Oh Lord, he thought, we are truly in a heap of trouble. Lord forgive us. When a preacher in a black suit comes to see you when it ain't Sunday afternoon either somebody's died or you're truly in a heap of trouble. And for him to come all the way from Anthony..."

The Reverend Lee took off his hat, showing a shock of golden red hair. A broad smile showed a healthy crop of straight, white teeth and crinkled the freckles scattered across the bridge of his nose. "Mr. Starling, Mrs. Starling," he said, extending his hand toward Adrian and nodding toward Ruby. "We're all here to celebrate your fiftieth wedding anniversary-your golden anniversary."

Adrian shook the preacher's strong hand. "Well, Reverend, we appreciate that, but ...well...," Again he searched for the right words. "You see, we can't have no fiftieth anniversary, 'cause ...well, 'cause we ain't never been married proper like."

"Mister Starling, Robert told me about that. I want to assure you that in my way of thinking and, I am sure, in the eyes of the Lord, you folks are just as married as if you had stood in front of a preacher in the biggest and finest church in this country. You exchanged vows on a Bible and you have lived up to those vows...and you've raised a mighty fine family. But, if you feel that you can't really celebrate because you haven't been officially married, I've come prepared. I'll need each of you to sign this paper and then I'll perform the ceremony right here on your front steps ...in front of all these witnesses, and then we'll have a real celebration!" He extended a paper and a fountain pen.

Adrian and Ruby looked out at the faces of their family members and their friends, faces that had blossomed from serious to smiling. The two whispered back and forth. Adrian looked up once to see Robert looking on with anticipation. They conferred and then scratched their names on the paper.

"Hallelujah." Reverend Lee shouted, waving his Bible in the air, "We're going to have a wedding right here and now!" He took his place on the porch and Adrian and Ruby stood facing him on the bottom step, Adrian on the right, Ruby on the left.

"Dear friends," the preacher began, "we are gathered here this evening..."

Adrian held up a hand. "Reverend...uh..."

"Lee," Ruby whispered, leaning toward Adrian.

"I know, dang it. Reverend Lee could you hold on for just a minute?"

Adrian climbed the steps, walked past Reverend Lee and went into the house. The friends and family members who had gathered close to hear the ceremony mumbled among themselves as they waited for Adrian to return.

He came back out the door a few minutes later carrying an old Bible, wrinkled from being carried in a saddlebag and stained with water from White Water Creek.

Adrian smiled at Ruby. "I thought we might want to hold this between us," he said, "just like we did fifty years ago."

The Winemakers

Neither Pop nor Jack, the black sharecropper who lived down the road with his common law wife, Cora, and their five children, knew anything about making wine, but when Jack found a wild fox grape vine lush with ripe little purple fruit they decided that they should give it a try. Pop sent Mom to town to buy sugar and cakes of yeast at the Piggly Wiggly store while he and Jack picked half a wash tub of grapes and then sat in the back yard under the big mulberry tree and mashed the fruit using clean Coca-Cola bottles as pestles.

They mixed the juice and pulp with the sugar and the yeast in a big pressure cooker Mom used to can Mason jars of fresh fruit and vegetables, and poured the thick mix into six one-gallon Coca-Cola syrup jugs that Pop had brought home from the open air soda shop next to the Ritz theater where Pop worked. They pulled dime-store balloons over the tops of the jugs, because that's what the assistant manager at the theater told Pop you had to do to keep in the gas that was generated as the mix fermented.

Jack took three of the jugs to his house and Pop put the other three in the kitchen next to the kerosene cook stove because the assistant manager, who seemed to know about such things, told him that the heat from the stove would make the mix ferment faster.

A week or so later we had to make a trip to St. Petersburg to pick up Grandma, a devout teetotaler who had no use for alcohol nor anybody who imbibed it in any form, for her annual summer visit. Pop decided that he had best hide the wine makings from view and, because he knew that Grandma had a nose that was acutely sensitive to any kind of alcoholic beverage, pulled off the balloons and screwed the Coca-Cola caps on the jugs, turned the dresser in his and Mom's bedroom sideways in the corner and hid the jugs behind it beside the old twelve-gauge that he always kept loaded but never hunted with because he didn't like to kill things.

Pop made arrangements for Jack to feed the chickens and cows for a few days and the six of us, including Tom, the cat, and Flash, the dog, left in the '34 Ford for the trip that took nearly all day, one way. My brother Charlie sat in front with Pop and I sat in back with Mom, Tom and Flash. I sat on Pop's handkerchief because the stiff brownish-gray "mouse fuzz" upholstery began to irritate the backs of your legs after you sat on it for a while in short pants.

We stayed in "St. Pete" for a few days to visit with Aunt Edie, Uncle Clark, the O'Berrys and the Pyles and left early Wednesday morning with Mom, my brother Charlie, Tom and Flash and sacks of mangoes, avocados and guavas in the back seat and Pop, me and Grandma in the front seat because Grandma said she always got "giddy" if she rode in the back seat. Flash rode next to the window in the back seat with his head poked out in the wind like he always did until one day a few months later when he snapped at a bush growing beside the road to our house, hung on and disappeared out the window.

The cooter shell trunk was loaded with boxes and bags of things that Mom and Pop had bought at Montgomery Ward and at Kress five and ten cent store where my brother Charlie and I begged to go down the wide marble steps with the big, round, brass handrail to the toy department that was twice the size of the toy department in the McCrory's in our town. Grandma's suitcases were wrapped in oil cloth, in case of rain, and tied to the car between the fender and the hood.

In Wildwood, at a Texaco station, my brother Charlie and I watched, fascinated, as a boy, not much older than my brother pushed and pulled a long handle back and forth to fill the big glass bowl at the top of the gas pump to the five-gallon mark and then drained it into the tank of the '34 Ford. After we all went to the restrooms, Pop fished "Cokes" out of a bright red cooler filled with cold water and chunks of ice and we drank the "Cokes" and played "travel" by checking the bottoms of the bottles for the names of the towns the bottles came from to see whose was the farthest away.

Long before we got home everybody was irritable from traveling in the summer heat and smelling dead cows that had fallen victim to cars traveling through the open range country. I had squirmed off Pop's handkerchief and Grandma had taken off her summer straw hat. She dabbed at her face and neck with a lace-trimmed hanky and fanned herself with a cardboard church fan that had a picture of Jesus printed on one side and an advertisement for Wilhelm's Funeral Home on the other.

When we got to the house everybody loaded themselves with boxes or bags or suitcases except Grandma who went ahead to "hold the door," for everybody else, all the while declaring that she felt she would surely perish if she didn't soon get a glass of cold water from the big bottle that was always in the ice box.

Grandma swung open the front door and stepped inside. A few minutes later the rest of us followed to find her sitting on the living room sofa, her summer straw hat back on her head and pinned to her hair and her big purse held tightly in her lap with both hands.

"I'm ready to go home," Grandma announced, looking straight ahead. "Never in my born days did I think I would ever walk into the home of my own flesh and blood and be confronted with that horrible odor!"

Tom and Flash were already sniffing the air when the rest of us suddenly became aware of the aroma of fermented grapes that permeated the house. At the age of seven I recognized the sour odor as wine only because I remembered it from the time, when I was four, that Pop and I got a little tipsy from a sample of sweet strawberry wine proffered by a neighbor down the road and Pop had mistakenly figured that such a clear, sweet drink would have little, if any, alcohol.

Pop disappeared toward his and Mom's bedroom and we heard him say, "Oh shoot," his favorite expletive when Grandma was around. Mom, my brother Charlie and I went to the bedroom to find out what was wrong to find Pop sitting on the side of the bed, his elbows on his knees and his chin cupped in his hands.

The wall behind and the ceiling above the dresser, the top of the dresser, the floor between the dresser and the bed and half of Mom's favorite chenille bedspread, that she had put on the bed especially for Grandma's visit, were covered with a thick, sticky mess of purple juice and Mom's free-standing full-length mirror that she had ordered from Sears Roebuck lay, smashed, on the floor.

After several minutes of Mom's exasperated pronouncements followed by her bundling up her favorite chenille bedspread and dashing to the Easy washer on the back porch, Pop moved the dresser away from the wall to begin the cleanup by taking out the three Coca-Cola jugs that had produced the sticky material when he stopped and again said, "Oh shoot."

My brother Charlie and I stepped around the dresser, our shoes sticking to the floor, to see what had caused Pop to use his favorite expletive, when Grandma was around, for the second time. What we saw was a hole about three inches across completely through the bedroom wall.

The summer heat had been a little too hot and the wine had "made" quicker than expected, building up a great load of gas in the process. The pressure of the gas had blown the tops off the Coca-Cola jugs with a force strong enough to spray juice like a small volcano. The purple eruption had knocked the shotgun down and the impact had caused both loads to discharge with the muzzles flush against the wall, the push of the explosions rocketed the gun across the room. It knocked down Mom's free-standing, full-length mirror that she had ordered from Sears Roebuck.

Grandma didn't stay as long as she usually did on her annual summer visits. She had Mom drive her to the Western Union office in town and she sent a telegram to Uncle Clark telling him to meet her at the railroad station at third street and second avenue south...as though he didn't know where the one railroad station was in St. Petersburg...and she took the Seaboard Railroad train home two days later.

She didn't say much to Pop during her short stay, but Mom said Grandma had never really liked Pop since before Mom and Pop were married when Grandma had seen Pop take butter from the butter dish with his table knife instead of the butter knife.

A week or so after Grandma went home, Jack strained the fermented mix from his three jugs and brought Pop one of them. The two of them sat on the back steps, sampling the sweet, grape wine and laughed about their first experience at wine making, and Pop said he guessed he was going to have to order a chenille bedspread and a free-standing, full-length mirror from Sears Roebuck.

Stand Up

"Help me, damn you! You can't jus' sit there and let me drown!"

Billy Shoemaker shifted his perch on the back fender of the old Studebaker that rested on its side in the river. He wiped away the water that ran from his dark hair into his eyes.

"D-Don't think I could d-do that, P-Pa," Billy shouted to the man who was holding onto a thin branch that hung low enough for him to grab as the current had taken him downstream away from the car. "D-Don't reckon I c-could do it the r-right way... or the way you'd want me to do it. I d-don't ever do anything right for you. Don't want to chance d-doin' something wrong and g-gettin' stropped for it."

"Damn you! I can't swim! Help me!"

The sixteen-year-old watched as his father flailed the air and the water with his free hand. The current lifted the man's feet to the surface and he kicked with such ferocity that one high-top brogan flew into the air and clunked down against a log that sloped down the bank into the water, causing three Slider turtles to leap from their sunning spots and splash into the cold brown water.

"Reckon you're just g-gonna have to d-do what I'm d-doin 'll

"You ain't doin' nothin', just sittin' there. Get me out of here!" The man's lips were blue and his teeth were chattering from the cold water.

"I'm s-standing up. I'm sitting here, but I'm standing up."

Stand up. That's what Mr. Squires at the feed store had told Billy he had to do. Stand up.

"You've got to stand up for yourself," Mr. Squires had said. "Stand up."

Mr. Shoemaker had been shouting at his son when they had driven down the alley behind Squires' Feed Store and he backed the old car in close to the loading dock. Billy sat in the car with his head down until his father opened the passenger-side door and grabbed the boy's arm.

"Y-Yessir."

"Damn. When you gonna learn to talk right. Bu-bu-bu. Damn. Can't even talk without all that bu-bu-bu."

Mr. Shoemaker walked through the storeroom to the front of the store and ordered the feed and fertilizer he needed, addressing Mr. Squires in his usual gruff, impatient manner.

Father and son started loading the bags into the back of the car where the seat had been removed to accommodate the load. Billy dropped a bag of feed into the back of the car with no greater drop than his father had dropped other bags, but the old man berated the boy, shouting that the he was going to bust them bags wide open, and that he could never do nothin' right and that he was never going amount to nothing.

He glowered at the boy and drew back his hand. Mr. Squires moved between the two. He said nothing, but the motion of his heavy body and the cold green eyes that cut into Shoemaker's said enough. Shoemaker stopped and looked into those eyes and lowered his hand. He looked at the man and then back at Billy. "You stay here," he said, "I'm goin' up to the square. You stay right here. I don't want to have to go huntin' all over this damn town for you when I'm ready to go home." He walked away, and then turned. "Don't go nowhere," He walked around the corner of the store and down the dirt alley.

Billy watched his pa turn toward Main street. Toward the Brass Rail bar. He knew that it would be more than an hour before the man would return his breath heavy with the sour odor of whiskey. And the whiskey always seemed to make him find more things wrong with Billy.

He went to the car and took his geography text from under the front seat where he had hidden it from his father. He went into the storeroom and sat on the top of a stack of bags of sweet-smelling citrus pulp cow feed and opened the book to the pages assigned to be read by Monday.
The long waits for his father to return didn't bother Billy. In fact, it was one of the times he enjoyed. One of the times along with the hours spent in school and Sunday mornings when he, his mother and his sisters would walk down the dirt road to church, and the times when he would walk deep into the woods below the farm where he would sit with his back against the trunk of a huge oak and read the books his father had little use for. Times when he would be away from the harsh attacks of his father. Times when he savored the quiet and could think about things or read and not be accused of wasting time or lallygagging.
He had read only a few pages of his geography assignment, carefully making notes on a folded sheet of notebook paper, when Mr. Squires came and sat down close beside him. Squires took off the hat that seemed to Billy to be as much a part of the man's head as his bushy eyebrows or his heavy-lobed ears. He wiped the sweat band of his hat and then the top of his bald head with a wrinkled, damp handkerchief, put the hat back on and pushed it toward the back of his head.
"What are you reading, Billy?"
"G-Geography. R-Reading for school."
"You like geography?"
It was difficult for Billy to look directly at Mr. Squires or at any other grown up. He glanced at the man and quickly looked back at his book.
"Y-Yessir.   I like to read about all the p-places I've never been ...and I'm n-never likely to go."
"How are you doing in school?"

"Some A's. Mostly B-B's and C's. M-Mama says I'm doin' real g-good, but P-Pa says I oughta quit."

Squires looked at the boy and frowned. "Quit? Why should you quit? You're doing well in school."

"P-Pa says I don't need to know m-much to work around the farm. He says that's all I'll ever b-be good for."

"Don't you do it, Billy. You finish high school. Get all the education you can. I guess a body doesn't need much education these days. Not many jobs around, because of the depression, but Mr. Roosevelt's going to get us out of this and in the forties and fifties a man is going to have to have a high school education to get a good job."

"But P-Pa says..."

"Billy, you're about grown. Nearly as big as your daddy now. How long are you going to take the way he treats you?"

"He's m-my pa, and I..."

"He's your pa, that's right, but that doesn't give him the right to yell at you the way he does...or hit you. I know he beats you sometimes. I'm not going to say a lot against your pa, but you don't have to take the kind of treatment that you've been taking. Some day you got to have to stand up, Billy. You got to stand up for yourself."

Mr. Squires lifted his heavy body from the sack of feed and looked straight into Billy's eyes. "As for those places you read about, you get a good education and someday you just might be able to go see those places." Without taking his eyes off Billy's he took off his hat and wiped the sweat band and the top of his head again. "Stand up," he repeated, put on his hat and walked through the storeroom door toward the front of the store.

There was a lot of time for thinking before Billy's pa got back. A lot of time for thinking...and remembering the years of abuse that his father had directed at him, time for thinking that left little time for reading Geography. He couldn't remember a time his father had talked to him in a way that made him feel good. Gentle, kind, loving words. Never. Attention from his father had always come in the form of harsh words or from a stick or a razor strop or a fist. It seemed that from the time he was old enough to do things he had never done anything right--at least not right to his father's way of thinking.

Billy took the Geography book to the car and started to slide it under the seat so his father wouldn't see it, then changed his mind and placed it on the seat.

When he finally saw his father coming back down the dirt alley, his footsteps unsteady, his skinny shoulders hunched from his hands being pushed deep into the pockets of his overalls, his hat pulled low over his eyes and his face sullen and ruddy, Billy thought it best to get into the Studebaker before his pa got there. No use chancing the whiskey-charged wrath sure to come as the result of, "...makin' me wait 'round for you cause you warn't ready to go when I was." Billy climbed in and sat on the book.

Shoemaker started the car and forced the gear shift into first amid grinding and grating protests that emanated from beneath the car as the result of his not having pushed the clutch pedal fully to the floor. The grinding and grating noises from the transmission and the sputtering and coughing noises made by the engine when it balked against Shoemaker's unsuccessful attempts to coordinate the movements of the clutch and accelerator pedals were answered with loud, profane pronouncements as to the inferior quality and questionable ancestry of the vehicle.

Good thing old Studebakers don't have feelings, Billy thought ...or maybe they do and the noises and balking were the dependable old car's way of striking back...its way of standing up.

Billy's pa sat stiff and leaned forward in the seat and squinted through the flat, dusty windshield as he maneuvered the car along the narrow hard road toward home.

The car roamed left and right across the road, but it hardly mattered because there was little traffic going either way. Most of the people who went to town on Saturday afternoon were already there and weren't yet ready to go home.

Billy sat close against the door of the car, one hand braced against the dashboard, the other gripping the edge of the seat. As the car neared the old single-lane, Sharpes Ferry wood-and-rusty-steel bridge over the spring-fed Ocklawaha, Billy realized the discomfort of sitting on a hard Geography book. He raised himself slightly and pulled out the book, hoping that his pa was too drunk or too busy driving to notice.

The car lurched over a pothole. The heavy book slipped from Billy's hand and banged against the floorboard of the car.

"What the hell was that?"

Billy scrambled to retrieve the book. "My b-book... my Geography book." Billy held up the book for his father to see.

"You got no need for no damned geography book! I tol' you...you gonna quit school an' help me out 'round the place! Gimme that damn book!" He grabbed the book from the boy's hand and threw it out the window. Billy lunged to save the book and hit the steering wheel. Shoemaker's foot shoved the accelerator to the floor.

The car swerved violently. It veered to the left and tipped up on the right wheels as it started across the bridge. Rusted steel twisted, bolts ripped from splintering wood and the car tore through the sagging guardrail. It snagged against a piece of metal and twisted in the air before splashing into the cold water eight feet below the bridge and settling on its right side onto the soft sand bottom.

After a time, Shoemaker's head appeared through the left front window, then his neck, shoulders and body being pushed by Billy's hands, Billy still submerged inside the car. The man clambered through the window with Billy's help, then lost his balance as he tried to get to his knees and fell off the car headfirst into the river.

He bobbed to the surface spitting water, coughing, and wind milling his arms in an attempt to stay afloat. The current carried him downstream some fifty feet before his head scraped against the low-hanging branch which he grabbed more as a reflex than as a conscious effort to save himself.

"Help me, damn you! You can't jus' sit there and let me drown!"

"D-Don't think I could d-do that, P-Pa. Don't reckon I c-could do it the r-right way ...or the way you'd want me to do it. I d-don't ever ever do anything right for you. Don't want to chance d-doin' something wrong and g-gettin' stropped for it."

"Damn you, I can't swim. Help me!"

"Reckon you're gonna have to d-do what I'm d-doin'."

"You ain't doin' nothin', just sittin' there. Get me out of here!"

"I'm standing up. I'm sitting here, but I'm standing up."

Billy slipped into the water and swam to the shore, stepped out of the water and onto the steep bank. He climbed the rest of the way up the bank using the torn, rusty handrail that was bent nearly to the angle of the sandy slope.

"You're gonna burn in hell for lettin' me drown this way!" he heard his father shout. "The Bible says you're supposed to save your father...and mother. Damn you. Help me!"

Billy looked back toward his father. He had fished the river around the bridge and swum in the cold, brown water. He knew the depth of the river where his father clung to the branch. "Stand up", he said in a loud voice. "Just stand up." He stood with his hands on his hips and looked at his father for a time, then shook his head, turned, and started walking slowly toward town, searching the weeds that bordered the road for a book about countries he thought he would never see.

* * * * *

Less than a decade later Billy got to see some of the countries he had read about: England, Ireland, Scotland, Belgium, Holland, France. The last time he stood up, he had a machine gun in his hands.

When You're a Man

Eighteen dollars and sixty-three cents in a wad of bills and coins, the key to a ten-year-old Dodge, a double-bladed Case knife and two-thirds of a plug of Brown's Mule chewing tobacco. Not much to show for the life of a man like Camp Hartley who had worked hard all his life.

Of course, there were forty acres of pretty good land, the house and out buildings, the animals and the old Dodge that Camp Hartley had cleared and planted, built, raised, and kept running, but there were few personal effects left behind. That was like him, though, more interested in providing all he could for his family than acquiring things for himself.

Tad Hartley looked at the things on the top of the chest of drawers. He opened the double bladed knife and tested the edge with his thumb. Sharp enough to shave. "Sharp blade is safer than a dull blade," Daddy Camp had always said, "Dull blade can slip and cut you easier than a sharp blade if it's not handled right." He had bought Tad a single blade Case when Tad was six, and taught his son how to sharpen it and how to use it. Tad could feel its weight in the left pants pocket of the new wool suit from J.C. Penney.

The first suit he ever had and it was heavy and too warm here in the house and a little too big with the coat sleeves hanging too far past his wrists. He didn't care that his mama had told him he would grow into it; he wanted to rip it off. It and the new, low cut black shoes, and the starched white shirt with the stiff collar that scraped his neck and the tie that was about to cut off his breath. Rip them off and never wear them again, because they would always remind him of the stuffy warm church and his mama and his sisters crying and how badly he had wanted to cry too, but couldn't because men don't cry, and the preacher had told him that he was the man of the house now, and how the people had sung hymns ...sad hymns... that didn't sound right without Daddy Camp's rich tenor, and how they had lowered the plain wood coffin into the hole with ropes and shoveled the cold winter dirt on top of it. Rip the clothes off and never wear them again.

Brown's Mule. Daddy Camp had chewed it, but only when he was plowing or doing chores, or was away from the house. Never in the house. And when he would come in for dinner or supper or at the end of the day he would spit out the tobacco and stop at the pump to wash his mouth, swishing the cool water about and spitting it out two or three times until his mouth was clean, and then he would reach a tin on a shelf on the back porch and pop a clove bud into his mouth and chew it before he went into the house and gave Nell Hartley a hug and a kiss. Which he always did.

"Daddy Camp, Why do you do that? Why do you spit out water and then eat those little pieces of wood?" Tad had asked when he was seven.

"Some ladies don't like the smell or taste of tobacco. Your momma don't. I respect her for it, so I wash out my mouth and I chew cloves 'cause they make my breath smell real sweet and your mamma likes that."

"Daddy Camp, I want to chew some of that chewing tobacco. Can I?"

Camp wiped the pump water from his chin and crunched a clove as he sat down beside Tad on the edge of the back porch. "Tad, I know you see me chewing tobacco and a lot of other people you know, and some of them not much older than you, but I ain't real sure that it's good for young'uns. It's best you wait till you're grown. When you're a man, then you can try it."

Whenever Tad mentioned chewing tobacco, Daddy Camp always said the same thing, "When you're a man."

As he grew, Tad learned to walk like his father, swing an axe like his father, work a shovel like his father, talk like his father, to do so many things like his father, but there were two things he couldn't do...chew Brown's Mule like his father and drive the old Dodge like his father.

Must have been about eight years old, Tad remembered, coming home on Saturday afternoon from their trip to town. He had been sitting quietly in the back seat of the old Dodge, between his younger sisters thinking about it ever since he had watched his father and the other men sitting on the low wall around the Courthouse square talking about their farms and the problems of the world.
"How do you all do that, Daddy Camp?"
"Do what?"
Tad leaned his elbows against the top of the front seat between his parents. "How do you all chew tobacco and eat peanuts at the same time without either swallowin' the tobacco or spittin' out the peanuts?"
Camp Hartley laughed so hard he had trouble steering, and the Dodge jumped to one side and then the other as he laughed and slapped the wooden steering wheel with his big, work-rough hands.
"Tad, that's a good one, boy. I guess I never thought about it. It's just one of those things grown ups do. Saints preserve us, I'll probably never be able to eat boiled peanuts and chew Brown's Mule again. It's for certain if I think about doin' it, I'll end up swallowin' juice and spittin' peanuts."
Two weeks later, when the family was in town, Tad watched his father and other farmers sitting on the low wall around the Courthouse chewing tobacco and eating peanuts at the same time as they talked. And he felt his face prickle red when he heard Daddy Camp tell the others about Tad's questioning how they did that and they all turned to look at him sitting on the low wall and they all laughed.
Tad felt in the pocket of his overalls to make sure he still had the twenty cents he had earned delivering eggs and quart Mason jars of fresh milk to Miss Tillery. He walked around the square until he found Mr. Simmons, the crippled

old man who hobbled around the Courthouse square selling nickel sacks of boiled and parched peanuts from a basket hooked over his arm.

Tad held out a nickel. "Boiled, please, Sir.

Mr. Simmons took the coin and handed Tad the damp paper sack of peanuts. He said nothing, only grunted. Tad was relieved. He had always been a little afraid of the short, heavy man who wore his stained old felt hat low over his heavy brow and rolled from side to side as he leaned on his home-made cane and walked around the square selling his nickel sacks.

Tad waited for a Model "A" to pass and then crossed Main Street to the A&P grocery and made a purchase.

It was twenty minutes later when Camp Hartley turned around just in time to see his son suck a boiled peanut and its salty juice out of the shell, chew a few times, and squirt a stream of lumpy brown liquid onto the sidewalk. He got up and walked to where Tad sat and lowered himself onto the curb beside his son.

"Tad, what are you doing back here?"

"I'm learnin' how to eat boiled peanuts and chew at the same time like you do." Tad sucked another peanut, chewed, and spewed more brown liquid mixed with half-chewed peanut.

"You know what I told you about chewin' tobacco. I told you I didn't think it was good for young folks and that you was to wait. When you're a man...grown...then you can decide on whether you want to chew or not. Besides, if you swallow some of that tobacco juice...and you're most likely to...its goin' to make you mighty sick."

"Liguish."

"What? What are you saying? Your mouth is so full I can't make it out."

"Liguish. It's liguish I'm chewin', not 'bacco."

"Liguish? You mean it's licorice you're chewin', not tobacco?"

"'essir. It spits jus' like 'bacco. But I keep spittin' out peanut."

Daddy Camp looked away from the boy and put his hand over his mouth to stifle a laugh then turned back toward Tad. "Well, I don't reckon I can fault you for chewin' licorice, now can I? I used to like it myself. And I used to spit and pretend it was tobacco juice, too. Guess most boys do that sometimes. But I don't remember trying to chew licorice and eat boiled peanuts at the same time."

That had been the sum of Daddy Camp's comment about Tad's attempt to emulate his father. An hour later he had stopped the car just across the Sharpes Ferry bridge at the artesian well that chunked and clunked and pumped out cold sulphur water, and he and Tad had walked out the old planks to the green growth-coated well where he had gently bathed the boy's face with his handkerchief dipped in the cold water because Tad had become sick when a belly-full of sweet licorice and salty boiled peanuts protested most vehemently the bouncing of the old Dodge along the rough road.

Tad picked up the key to the old Dodge. It showed its age as surely as did the old car, rough and worn with only a few shiny spots. Daddy Camp had let Tad turn the key and press the starter with his foot sometimes when Tad was younger. And a month ago, just after Tad had turned fifteen, he had let Tad sit behind the wheel and start the car and try coordinating the brake, clutch, accelerator and the gear shift that stuck up from the floor. There had been strange grinding noises, jerks and jumps and the engine stalled. By the third time Daddy Camp had let him drive down the two-rut dirt road as far as the hard road. The grinding noises were shorter lived and not as loud, the old Dodge had only jerked and jumped a couple of times and the engine had quit only once. That had been the extent of Tad's driving before Saturday just past.

"C'mon Tad, let's get breakfast and take care of the stock so we can get to the feed store early," Daddy Camp had urged his son who was just rolling out of his warm bed. Then he smiled and added, "I'll let you drive to the hard road, and you can drive back from the hard road...if you promise not to mess up our beautiful car."

"Yes,,sir. I'm coming," Tad said, his feet dancing on the cold floor as he pulled on a flannel shirt, overalls and heavy work shoes. At fifteen he was already tall for his age and his body was muscular. With his quickly-combed blond hair falling down over his forehead and his faded farm clothes he looked like a smaller version of Camp Hartley...and nothing pleased him more than for someone to tell him so.

Nell Hartley had a big breakfast ready. A big, hot breakfast for a couple of men getting ready for hard work on a cold morning. Eggs with the white done and the yolk still soft the way Camp Hartley and Tad liked them, big brown patties of Nell's spicy-hot home made sausage, tongue-blistering hot grits, biscuits warmed from supper the evening before ready to be spread with fresh butter and topped with Mr Krazit's cane syrup, and plenty of hot coffee for Camp and fresh milk for Tad.

"Cold out there this morning," Nell said as she poured a second cup of coffee for her husband. "There's frost and it looks like there's ice on the water trough. Are you sure you want to go to the feed store so early? It'll warm up later in the day."

Camp blew on the coffee and took a sip. "I want to go and get finished early. Feel like just sitting in front of the fireplace and reading later on. Don't seem to have much get up and go this morning."

Camp and Tad finished their meal, pulled on heavy jackets and billed caps and took care of the morning chores.

Then they took the back seat out of the old Dodge to make room for two bales of hay and bags of cow and chicken feed.

Camp spit out his tobacco, rinsed his mouth with icy water from the pump, crunched a clove, hugged Nell, and kissed her good bye.

Tad drove to the hard road without stalling the engine at all and jumping the Dodge only twice when he shifted gears.

"That boy of yours is gettin' near 'bout big enough to wrestle you down, ain't he, Camp?" Mr. Squires, the owner of the feed store, teased as Tad and Daddy Camp loaded the hay and the feed into the back of the car. "Looks like he can throw 'round them bales of hay better than you can."

"I suppose he might think he is, but I don't think he's ready to try just yet. How about it Tad?"

"No, Sir, I don't think I'm ready to try that. Don't think I ever will be either."

"Sometimes he thinks he's ready to try a chew of tobacco," Camp said, "but I tell him when he's a man he can try it."

Tad looked at Daddy Camp. The weather was cold and the wind had a bite to it, but his father had pulled off his jacket and tossed it onto the front seat of the car. Circles of perspiration stained his shirt dark under the arms. As Tad watched, Camp leaned against the Dodge and wiped his forehead with his handkerchief.

They were half way home when Daddy Camp pulled the Dodge to the side of the hard road. He sat still for a time, his fist clenched against his chest. "Well," he said, "it looks as though your mama's sausage is a mite hot for an old man. It's talking back to me this morning. Got a belly ache like I've never had before." He wiped perspiration from his face and turned to Tad. "You want to drive home from here? I believe you're 'bout ready."

"Yes, Sir." Tad got out and left the door open for Daddy Camp to walk around from the driver's side. Instead, Camp slid across the seat and reached for the door. He stopped, straightened, and took a deep breath, reached again and pulled the door closed.

"Are you all right?" Tad asked. His father slid down in the seat and leaned his head against the door. Again he wiped his face with his handkerchief.

"Drive, Tad. Just drive on home. I'll be all right if you'll just get us on home so I can take a dose of baking soda. It's just that hot sausage of your mama's. I told her she was putting in too much pepper. Now you just stop your jabberin' and drive." He pressed his fist against his chest.

Daddy Camp's words startled Tad. He had never heard his father speak so harshly to anyone...not even to Betty, their old plow mule, when she got balky.

Tad moved the gearshift and the car jerked back onto the hard road when he lifted his foot off the clutch too quickly. He drove as fast as he dared, steering the old Dodge with both hands gripping the heavy wood steering wheel. He slowed the car when he turned off the hard road onto the two-rut dirt road, and again when he reached the Sharpes Ferry bridge. The old steel and wood structure moaned and rattled as the car moved slowly across the span.

They passed the artesian well, and Tad could hear the noises of the pump and he could smell the boiled-egg odor of the sulphur water.

"Tad, I'm sorry I talked to you that way," Daddy Camp said softly. "Had no right to ...just...just let the way I feel get the best of me, I guess. I'm sorry. His head still rested against the door, and his eyes were closed tight.

Tad looked at his father. "It's O.K.," he said. "Daddy Camp, are you real sure you're all right?"

"Yes, it's better now." Camp Hartley took a deep breath and let it out slowly. "Better."

Tad pulled off the J.C. Penney suit and the stiff shirt, tossed them on his bed, and kicked the new, low-cut black shoes under the bed. He put on a fresh work shirt and clean overalls from the chest of drawers and pulled on his heavy, high top work shoes. He left the eighteen dollars and sixty-three cents in bills and change on the chest of drawers. It was rightfully his mama's, he thought, not his. He picked up the key to the old Dodge and then put it back beside the money. Driving didn't interest him so much any more. Tad put the two-blade Case knife and the Brown's Mule in his pocket, picked up his ninth-grade school books, took them into the living room and left them on a table beside the front door. His sisters could take them to school tomorrow... or the next day.

Tad put on his jacket and did the evening chores, then climbed up a big spoked wheel and settled into the seat of the field wagon where he had sat beside Daddy Camp so many times. He looked at the comfortable farm house. Smoke from the living room fireplace and the kitchen stove filled the crisp evening with the aroma of burning oak. He looked at the old Dodge, the outbuildings, the cows and the chickens and Betty, the mule, and out across the forty acres of pretty good land.

Tad reached into the pocket of his overalls and took out Daddy Camp's two-blade Case knife and two-thirds plug of Brown's Mule and sliced off a piece.

Dreams of a sixteen-Year-Old

I watched her there asleep on the sofa,
Her breathing slow and deep.
Her head moved,
A small but sudden movement.
More movement,
Now her mouth.
A dream.
A good dream?
Eyes moving under twitching lids.
What was her dream?
Pleasant?
Sweet?
Fearful?
Her feet moved
Small movement
Now more.
Dancing or running?
Runing away?
Running to something desirable?
Something drawing her nearer?
Something she wants?
She wakes suddenly.
Escaping from imagined danger?
She stretches,
Limbering tense muscles.
She looks at me,
Her eyes blinking away sleep.
She comes to me and settles in my lap,
Reaches and touches my cheek
Gently,
Lovingly,
And starts to purr.

The Hitchhiker

The thin, spidery arms clung to me, tiny hook-like fingers digging into my clothing...clinging to me, begging to become part of my life and stay with me forever. I looked down at the tiny being and I understood its hunger for attachment to a person, bigger, stronger...its desire to be transported to a place it could claim as home, a place where it could put down roots and grow and prosper. '

"I understand your need," I said, "but our differences would never permit us to live together in harmony. You are so young, so sharp, but I am old and when I look at you I compare and realize that my life is pointless."

I reached down and tried to pull loose the grasping fingers. "Please," I pleaded, "let me go. Find another who will be more compatible with your needs. I am not right for you."

I tried again. As I freed myself from the tight grip a tiny stiletto flashed and pain seared my hand. A stain of blood appeared. "Damn you! Damn you," I shouted, "you care nothing of me, you only wanted what I could give you...a free ride! "Damn you. Damn you, you little...you little clinging, grasping, hurtful being. It's no wonder that no one loves you... you treacherous little sandspur!"

The Last of the Red-hot Marbles

1 935

     Dyer's red store wasn't much of a place. Just a four-room frame house on a graded dirt road till Casper Dyer reasoned that 'cause there weren't no stores anywhere in walking distance that he'd wall up half of the front porch and make it into a little store, and he'd drive his truck to town once a week and stock up on light bread, salt, sugar, flour, corn meal, dried beans, grits, pork and beans, sardines, and some other canned stuff and later on, corn plasters, liniment, BC or Stanback headache powders and other things folks 'round that part of the woods might need. After a couple years the stuff he sold took over the living room and the front bedroom and Mariah Dyer said she couldn't take it no more...people wanderin' through her house all day... so Casper built another house behind the first one to live in and bought a used pool table with fuzzed up felt, a set of chipped balls and four almost straight cue sticks and put them in the back bedroom of what was then all store, where, 'cause the floor wasn't quite level, Zero Toops, who shot pool more than anybody else, said it was easier to make a shot headed northwest than one headed southeast.

     Year or so later the Woco-Pep people talked Dyer into burying a big gas tank in the ground and a pump out front. Then the Coca-Cola folks paid him to let them paint the whole store Coca-Cola red an' paint Coca-Cola down both sides in big letters; that's how it come to be called Dyer's red store. And then somebody from Chattanooga put "See Rock City" in big black an' white letters on the roof.

     Folks that was at the store that afternoon took little notice when that scrawny little old man came in and bought a can of Vienna sausages, a single-row box of Uneeda crackers and an Orange Crush. Couldn't have stood more than five-foot-tall and had gnarled up hands that looked like they was 'bout twice as big as they should have been hangin' at the ends of them skinny arms. He had a beard down to 'bout here and it and what little hair he had under that cloth cap that sloped down toward the front like Yankees wear was about as white as anybody's you ever saw. His pants and shirt and plaid suit coat with a belt across the back were clean but wrinkled up like maybe he had washed them in the river and then hung them out on some bushes to dry while he washed hisself and his underwear. He was totin' a couple of croaker sacks tied together at the necks so he could carry them slung over his shoulder.

Well, that little old man set out on the front steps diggin' them Vienna sausages out of the can with the pointed blade of a pocket knife--his fingers was too big to dig down into the can--and eatin' them and those Uneeda crackers and drinkin' his Orange Crush, not sayin' nothin' to nobody. Then he heard Zero Toops and Dooley Cass clacking pool balls together. He stopped for a minute in his eatin' and listened to them balls clackin' and ate the rest of them sausages and crackers pretty near fast as he could and washed them down with the last of the Orange Crush.

That ol' fellow walked slow like back through the store half carryin' and half dragging them croaker sacks. He had his head stuck out so that with his pointed nose and long skinny neck and that white beard and hair he looked like a White Leghorn chicken sneakin' up on a bug.

He walked real quiet into the back bedroom...or the BILLIARD PARLOR as the sign said that Casper Dyer had talked the Coca-Cola sign painter into making for him... and sat down in a straight back, cane-bottom chair next to the door and watched Zero and Moody finish a game of eightball.

Moody dropped a dime into a Hav-A-Tampa cigar box on a table in the corner and tossed a nickel on the pool table. Zero picked it up, stuffed it in his pocket and started racking the balls for another game, and then he stopped and looked at that little old man like it was the first time he had noticed him.

"Wanta shoot a round?" he says to the old man, "Don't cost but five cent each a game and we usually make a nickel side bet. Loser pays for the game."

"I'm sorry," that little old man says, soundin' like some high educated northern type, "I haven't had the opportunity to enjoy the diversion of billiards in a number of years, so I have probably lost what little skill I had attained. Also, my pecuniary resources are rather limited at this time. Mr. Hoover's depression has taken its toll."

Nobody was quite sure what he was talkin' about at first with them big words and that Yankee accent. Boston, most likely. Nobody can understand people from Boston but other people from Boston.

Zero wasn't going to let on he wasn't sure what the old man had said, so he says, "Wanta shoot a round?" again. "Ain't but a nickel each and a nickel side bet. Come on, I ain't much of a pool shooter myself."

Now me and Moody was startin' to feel sorry for the old fellow 'cause he was beginnin' to look interested and he had dug some change out of his pants pocket, and me and Moody knew that Zero was so slick he could steal the heart out of a watermelon you was holdin' with both hands without leavin' a mark on the rind.

The old fellow says, "Well, I suppose I could take a few minutes... as I said, it has been some time..."

When Zero Toops laughed he sort of snorted through his nose. He laughed that way and the old fellow looked at him and asked if he was "quite well" and that made Zero snort some more when he said he was o.k., 'cause he could see that old fella paying for a few games and handing over nickels.

Zero was right in his thinking. He let the old man break all four games and the old man got two balls twice and Zero skunked him twice. Somehow, I kept feeling that old fellow could have made some of the shots that he missed...if he'd really wanted to.

After they finished the fourth game and the old man had put another dime in the Hav-A-Tampa box and handed Zero another nickel he mumbled something about being out of practice. Then he looked straight at Zero. "I don't suppose you would give me the opportunity to regain my losses by pitting wits over a chess board...or perhaps cribbage...backgammon?"

I guess he could read Zero's expressions well enough to see that Zero didn't know nothing about them games. He sort of sighed and bent over and picked up his croaker sacks and started to heist them over his shoulder when he stopped and looked at Zero again and said, "Marbles?"

Zero's face lit up like the neon sign out in front of the Ritz Theater, and he snorted through his nose again. Moody and me looked at one another and Moody shook his head just a little. Back when we was all kids--before Zero quit school after the sixth grade--Zero would clean us out at marbles...everything but our favorite shooters. We could beat most of the other kids, but Zero always won, and he always played for keeps.

"Well now," Zero says with another snort, "I used to be a pretty fair marble shooter back when I was a boy, but I ain't shot marbles in a long time. Course I ain't got no marbles now. My boy took them to school and them he didn't lose to other marble shooters the teacher took away from him. Boys don't shoot marbles much anymore, got too many other things to do. If we had some marbles, I'd say we'd have us a game."

"Oh, you are quite right. The youth of our great land no longer find satisfaction in getting down on their knees in the sand and playing a simple game. Now their interests are in football, air rifles, Saturday western matinées at the cinema and listening to the adventurous antics of pseudo-heroes as aired over the radio waves. Well now," that old fellow says, "Just let me have a look in my burlap luggage. I may have saved some prized aggies, moonstones and cat's eyes from my early years...ah yes, here they are. If you are so inclined, let us retire to the outdoors and find a suitable location for a ring. I believe I saw two or three dusty bags of marbles for sale in Mr. Dyer's emporium, if you'd like to purchase a bag I'm sure Mr. Dyer would let you have them at a reasonable price." The old man held up a soft leather bag with a drawstring and shook it. When them marbles inside that bag clinked together Zero Toops just couldn't hold back.

The game drew a pretty fair crowd. There was me and Moody and Mr. Dyer and his wife, the Mulkey twins that had walked to the red store for a loaf of light bread for supper, three boys and a girl that just got off the truck used for a school bus and a whole family of moss pullers that had stopped by to fill up a couple of Mason jars with water from the pump behind the red store.

The old man took a stick and scratched a circle in the sand. Must have been ten feet across. Biggest marble ring any of us had ever seen. Then he drew two lines across from one another touching the edge of that big circle. "That's the lag line," he says, "and this is the pitch line. We will, of course, abide by the rules as set down by the National Marble Tournament Committee." He took some of the marbles that Zero had just bought and with some of his own made a cross in the middle of that big circle...seven marbles in each direction. When he shook those marbles out of his bag into his overgrown hand everybody kind of gasped and crowded close to see them better. They was the prettiest, shiniest marbles anybody had ever seen.

"Oh." that old fellow says, "So you like these. Many of them are from West Virginia where most of our domestic marbles are manufactured; on the other hand these aggies are made of special, fine-grained quartz in Oberstein, Germany, as you undoubtedly know." Everybody mumbled and nodded their heads as if they already knew all that. Then he went to talking about a bunch of rules that nobody understood, using words like bowling, and histing, and lofting, and edgers. That should have been a tip off to Zero that he wasn't dealin' with some amateur that didn't know his way around a marble ring and hadn't been on his knees in the sand since he was a boy. But Zero always was a touch pig-headed and whenever he thought he had a chance of taking somebody for a little money, he just lost all his reasoning.

"Here," the old man says, "is a booklet of rules for your edification." He handed Zero a little hard-back book 'bout a half inch thick and stood there looking at Zero real solemn like.

Zero leafed through that little book and looked at the old man and the ring in the sand with a blank look on his face. It appeared that he was finally beginnin' to realize that he had been out snookered for the first time in his life. He stammered like I'd never heard him before and he kind of weak like says, "Are we p-playing for k-keeps?"

"Most certainly," the man says. "For keeps, and for fifty cents a game side bet as well, Mr. Toops. And I believe we will be able to complete our matches without obligation to Mr. Dyer's cigar box. The first contestant to shoot seven marbles outside the ring wins that game. Shall we begin Mr. Toops? Stand here with your toes to the pitch line and pitch to the lag line across the ring. The closer of the two wins"

Zero turned pale when he heard that man say, "...fifty cents a game side bet..." He reached in his bag of new marbles without looking and pulled out the first marble he could get his fingers on to use as his shooter. He knew pretty well, by then, that it didn't matter which marble he shot with. His hand was shakin' like a nervous pup.

He missed the lag line by a good foot. The old man's marble dropped on the line and stayed put like it growed there. General George A. Custer had a better chance with Sittin' Bull than Zero had against that fellow.

The old man dropped down on his knees like a twelve year old, got his head down real low with the end of his beard sweepin' at the sand, and squinted his left eye. That shooter tucked in between his thumb and finger looked like a BB in that big hand. He must have had the strongest thumb in the whole wide world. When he flicked it, that shooter would fly toward its target like a bullet, and when it hit, as it did every single time, it sounded like that smooth, round marble that got hit would shatter into little bitty pieces of sharp glass. But that marble would fly those five feet to the outside of that big ring and just keep agoin'. And when them marbles would ricochet around and hit a couple of other ones it would sound a lot like them pool balls clacking against one another.

    Zero never was one to give up. Ten times they pitched their shooters toward that lag line and ten times Zero just stood there with his shooter in his hand waitin' for his turn. After the last game Zero looked at me and then at Moody and we both just shook our heads. We learned a long time ago not to loan no money to Zero Toops, 'cause he never paid back money loans. He'd just want to shoot pool or pitch pennies or play high card for double or nothin' and when we was through he'd just snort that laugh through his nose and say somethin' like, "Now ain't that just too bad."

    Zero didn't say nothin'. He just dug down in his pocket and counted out four dollars and eighty-three cents including three soggy, wadded up dollar bills. "That's all I got," he says when he handed the old man the money. "Don't make much drivin' a dump truck out there where they're diggin' that cross Florida canal, and with my wife and my young 'uns we dont..."

    "That's quite all right, young man," the old man says. He dropped all his and Zero's marbles into his soft leather bag and put it and the little hard-back book of rules down in the bottom of one of the croaker sacks. Then he smoothed out the dollar bills, folded them real neat like and put them in his pocket. He tied the croaker sacks together, swung them over his shoulder and started down the graded dirt road. "If ever I should be fortunate enough to pass this way again I shall attempt to look you up and perhaps we will play for the seventeen cents...double or nothing."

When Florida Folks pulled the old man's beard---for a living

The words "Spanish moss" conjure--in some people's minds--images of stately, southern mansions surrounded by majestic oaks festooned with long, flowing strands of gray moss. To others who lived in Florida in the past, "Spanish moss" meant hours of arm-tiring, back-breaking labor that provided a meager living. From the early years of Florida history until the late 1950s, moss gathering and processing was an important industry in our state.

Spanish moss is sometimes referred to as southern moss, Florida moss, or "the old man's beard", but it is not a moss at all; it is a bromeliad. The most familiar plant of that family is the pineapple. Moss needs no roots; water is absorbed through its leaves and is then combined with carbon dioxide to manufacture food by photosynthesis. It is not a parasite; it uses the tree as an anchor, but it can harm a tree if it becomes so thick that it blocks out sunshine or breaks branches after heavy rains. It can absorb several times its own weight in water. During May and June tiny yellow-green flowers appear at the base of the slim leaves, but the seeds do not mature until the following March.

The plant is native to America, and probably came to be called "Spanish moss" because it grows in the areas first visited by Spanish explorers. In the early days, the settlers gathered the moss, cured and ginned it by hand and used the fibers to make braided ropes, bridles, saddle blankets, and as the padding in horse collars. After the turn of the century the finished material was recognized as a high--quality filler for mattresses, cushions, and pillows, and as cushioning for automobile and airplane seats. When properly prepared, it remained resilient for years, and was almost indestructible. An added advantage of using moss in upholstering furniture was that it did not attract insects.

Through the depression years and into the forties, moss gathering was a primary source of income for many families who pulled moss year round, and provided additional income for farm families during the winter months when farm work was slack. While visitors and newer residents of the state may know the silvery strands only for their aesthetic value, others have seen it as a source of survival during the lean years.

Moss was pulled from the trees using long, cane poles tipped with wire hooks. It was said that a good moss puller could gather 500 pounds of green moss a day, and a family of four could pull a ton. It is easy to imagine the many bottles of liniment that must have been used to soothe aching muscles after a day of stretching to lift the long, heavy poles to pull the moss from high in the trees. In many cases, almost all family members pitched in, the adults and older children pulling the moss and the younger children carrying it to the wagon or truck.

When the moss was hauled to the processing plants where it was graded and weighed, it brought only enough for a family to carry out a minimal existence. In the late fifties the plants paid about $14.00 a ton.

There were several methods of curing the moss, but a method called pitting was most often used. The moss was cleaned of sticks and trash, wet down thoroughly, and packed in trenches about four feet deep and four feet wide. After a few days, heat was generated. This moist heat rotted the bark and leaves from the core. After two or three months, the moss was turned over, the center of the pile pitched to the outside and the outside to the center. It was again soaked with water and left in the pits for another two or three months. When the soft, gray covering slipped from the tough, wiry core, the moss was taken from the pit and hung on lines to dry. The five to six month rotting process reduced the moss to about 25% of its original weight. So a ton of moss pulled from the trees provided only 500 to 700 pounds of cured material.

Ginning was the next step in the process. Any remaining sticks and trash were picked out by hand, the fibers were pulled apart and fed into the gin, a machine that further straightened the fibers. Inside the gin was a drum with protruding steel teeth that combed the fiber and pulled out any remaining debris as the drum turned at some 1200 times a minute. The fibers were then raked over a lattice work floor as a final cleaning and run through the gin a second time.

Because of loss during ginning, the final yield of black, wiry material amounted to only 15 to 20 percent of the weight of the moss taken from the trees.

In the mid-1930s, the prime years of the business, there were several dozen gins in Florida, but by the late 50's there were only two in operation; the Vego-Hair Manufacturing Company in Gainesville and the Florida Moss Ginning Company of Ocala. There are no records to tell us how much moss was processed during the peak years, but in 1925 moss production in the United States was 18,800,000 pounds with Louisiana first and Florida second in production. The industry thrived until the late 1950s when less expensive foam upholstering materials were invented. Not only has the moss pulling and processing business disappeared from the state, but now there are indications that the moss itself may follow. It is very sensitive to pollutants in the air which are readily picked up by the velvety surface of the moss. Scientists first saw that the moss was dying in Manatee County in 1968, and reports of moss being in trouble soon came from other areas of central Florida.

It would be difficult indeed to picture old southern mansions surrounded by stately oaks bare of the beautiful gray, flowing strands of "the old man's beard."

A Streetcar Called Jungle

It was big and yellow with a brown top and a headlight at each end like a giant, fat, yellow, two headed caterpillar.

It was a streetcar called "Jungle."

It rattled and clattered out St, Petersburg's Central Avenue from downtown by the shore of Tampa Bay west to a community named "The Jungle" by some developer with an odd sense of humor during Florida's building boom of the twenties.

When the motorman "opened 'er up" the electric-powered car would bounce along the tracks and oscillate rhythmically from side to side so violently we would have to hang on to the back of the seat in front of us to keep from being flung across the aisle.

The wires that fed electricity to the streetcars were strung high over the middle of the streets, creating a high-voltage web that covered the city.

When the streetcar reached the end of the line, the motorman would take the control lever to the other end of the car, flipping the backs of the seats as he passed, making the old back end the new front end. Then he would pull the electric trolley contact down at the old back end and raise the one on the old front end making it the new back end.

When the trolley crossed the intersection of two routes there would be a loud ZAP with a shower of sparks like the Fourth of July.

Many kids rode the streetcar to and from school, but for high school students, the streetcars were often their transportation for dates. Students got a special fare and boys carried coins in their "dime loafers" in case of an "emergency." They took their dates to the Florida, the La Plaza, the Playhouse or one of the other theaters to see such movies as "Carnival in Costa Rica," or that terribly obscene "The Outlaw" in which Jane Russell went as far as loosening the bow at her neckline and saying, I'll get you warm," to a handsome young cowboy who was suffering a life-threatening gunshot wound.

From home, I would walk a couple of blocks to Central Avenue and 25th Street, ride to 42nd Street, and walk two blocks to my girlfriend's house. We would walk back to Central, ride to 4th Street, see a movie, drop by Liggett's for a coke or "shake," maybe sit on a bench at Mirror Lake and…uh…talk for a while, then ride back to 42nd street and then I would ride back to 25th Street.

"Jungle" wasn't the only route, but the others didn't have glamorous names like "Jungle." They had names like Lealman, Gulfport, Pier, or 28th Street. "Jungle" is the one that brings back memories and reminds me of motorman Mr. Sims.

Mr. Sims was a Disney picture of a streetcar motorman. He was slim and stood several inches over six feet, had a handlebar mustache left over from the gay nineties when he surely had been a gay young blade. He wore black trousers, white shirt, black leather bow tie, shiny black shoes and a round, billed cap with a silver badge…the motorman's uniform in those days.

My girlfriend and I had been to a Friday night movie, had a coke at Liggett's, sat on a green bench by Mirror Lake and caught the last streetcar to Jungle.

We were the only passengers. When we got to 42nd Street Mr. Sims didn't open the door. He smiled at us and looked at my girlfriend.

"I've noticed that lately your boyfriend hasn't made it back from your house in time to ride back to twenty-fifth Street, and you know that when I come back, it's the last car for the night. That's a long walk near midnight. Not too safe and a couple of unlighted blocks along Goose Pond are kinda spooky."

"From now on, I'll blow the whistle at forty-seventh and slow down. You give him one last kiss and send him on his way. If he's coming this way, I'll wait."

After that he would toot the whistle at 47th, she would give that last kiss and I'd run toward Central Avenue....well, most of the time I'd run toward Central. Sometimes I still had to walk home.

We didn't have a car. Good used ones were hard to find during the war years, and gasoline was rationed. But we didn't need one; we had the streetcars. Dad rode the streetcars to work and back home and Mom took care of her shopping the same way. Some folks would ride to the pier carrying fishing gear and go home on the streetcar with their gear plus a string of fish.

The streetcar was an integral part of St. Petersburg for many years. They added a certain charm to the city.

True, we had to dash to the middle of the street avoiding oncoming traffic to get aboard and make the same dash to the curb when we got off....conditions that would not be tolerated under today's government-mandated safety regulations, but we just took those conditions for granted and raced back and forth.

Colored folks had to sit at the back of the car. Rediculous, not only from the standpoint of the stupidity of segregation, but from the fact that the back of the car was the front on the return trip.

The steel rails in the middle of the street posed a safety hazard when a drizzle of rain turned the steel rails with their coat of oily residue into a skating rink for drivers who tried to brake with all four tires on the rails.

A couple of years ago I went to St. Petersburg for a class reunion. What I found saddened me, but did not surprise me. The streetcars were gone. The tracks had been ripped up—the scars healed with asphalt paving. The web of wires that fed the trolleys had been torn away as though some giant bird had dived through a spider's web.

The streetcars were gone. In their place were diesel buses....noisy, fume spewing, smoke belching, heat-barfing diesel buses.

The "Jungle" route was no more. The buses that roared out Central Avenue, blocking the flow of traffic with its protruding rear when it nosed to the curb to take on or discharge passengers had some innocuous name like "150 Street."

Bus riders will never hear the streetcar bell ring or the whistle blow or be late for a date because some kid—on a dare—ran out and pulled the trolley pole off the wire.

I doubt that riders would be permitted aboard one of the diesel monsters with a string of fish caught from the pier…if they were permitted to fish from the pier…or if they ever caught anything if it were permitted.

I know for certain they will never ride with a kindly motorman with a handlebar mustache who cares enough about his riders to council a young lady to: "Give him one last kiss and send him on his way."

Made in the USA
Columbia, SC
24 March 2019